To June, m
with l
Jean.

CW01021350

# LITTLE JEAN'S WAR

*Jean Pearce Edwards*

Jean Pearce Edwards

authorHOUSE®

*AuthorHouse™*
*1663 Liberty Drive, Suite 200*
*Bloomington, IN 47403*
*www.authorhouse.com*
*Phone: 1-800-839-8640*

*First published by AuthorHouse  9/11/2008*

*ISBN: 978-1-4343-9133-9 (sc)*

*Printed in the United States of America*
*Bloomington, Indiana*

*This book is printed on acid-free paper.*

# Dedications

I would like to thank Gillian who listens and Barbara who can spell; as always they helped me in the early stages.

I lovingly thank my husband John who has to put up with my forgetting to cook dinner when I'm writing.

I dedicate this little book to my family members; Francesca my daughter, Christopher John Pearce Edwards, my son and last of the Pearce line and Megan my darling granddaughter.

Thanks too to Jacqueline, my goddaughter for loaning me Joyce's old photos.

To all my friends, old and new; I hope you enjoy this tale.

Jean has written three novels, Dreamkill, Dreamshatter and Homestar.

# Foreword

When I tell my children about my experiences during the war, I realise just how unbelievable it sounds to them. So I put pen to paper to record my memories so that my children Christopher and Francesca and my granddaughter, Meg can keep the memories alive and see how it was for my generation as we grew up during World War Two. We did not realise what we were missing; we could not remember much about life "before the war."

My children, having been born in the 60's, cannot imagine life without television, computers, junk food and even refrigerators. None of these things were available back then so I did not know what I was missing and it was no hardship.

One day there won't be any of us left of that generation and so I decided to weave a story around my memories.

Today's child may find it hard to believe that we could have such fun enjoying that simple country-style life.

I have decided to publish these memories because so many of my friends have asked me to do so.

I hope that you enjoy the story of little Jean, her cousins Frank and Joyce and of course Jean's cat Tubby.

# Tubby and Little Jean

The little girl was lying snug in her bed wrapped all around by her eiderdown. Her cat Tubby lay beside her, purring quietly and waiting for his special charge to wake up. She had been given into his care almost four years previously when he himself was just a little ginger kitten and they had been constant companions ever since. If a cat could think then that was the role he had assumed for himself anyway

Tubby sat up and began to wash his face. The movement disturbed little Jean and she rolled over and stretched. It was still dark on that late September morning in 1940 and the blackout curtain was pulled tightly down across the little attic window of Jean's bedroom. Gradually she began to awaken. She had a feeling that it was going to be a special day today. Suddenly she remembered why; her Aunt was coming down from London to see Jean's mother and Peter would be coming too with the new baby.

The child sat up in bed and threw off the covers. She ran over to the window and pulled back the blind a little crack. Please let it be a nice day today, she said to herself. It was still dark but it was not raining and there was no red glow on the horizon. Good she thought, we can go and play in the brickyard later on. Looking round she noticed that the covers on her bed were moving in an alarming way and some very odd noises were coming from beneath.

"Oops," she cried, rescuing a very disgruntled marmalade cat. Jean tried to give poor Tubby a cuddle but he was very put out and sauntered off towards the door where, turning his back on Jean in a very deliberate manner, he began to wash himself thoroughly.

"Please don't wash behind your ears, Tubby."

When a cat washes behind its ears it means that it will rain very hard before the day is over; but Tubby did wash behind his ears anyway, just to be awkward.

Jean began the laborious task of dressing herself. Her clothes lay scattered all across the floor of her large attic bedroom, just as she had left them the night before. She struggled to get her socks on the right way round but somehow the heels always managed to end up on the top of her foot and were very hard to turn around the right way again. She gave a large sigh when at last she was dressed and skipped across to the door. Her mum expected her to wash before dressing but Jean hated to go into the cold bathroom in her nighty. Tubby had finished washing himself and was doing his enormous stretch. Only cats can stretch themselves in such a peculiar way. Tubby's front legs stretched out before him, his bottom pointing upwards as his whole body grew longer and longer and then suddenly he shrunk back to normal again.

Jean slid down the banister on the staircase which led into the kitchen. Tubby bounded down the stairs to meet her at the bottom. This was their routine of the day.

In the bathroom Jean decided that it would be much nicer if she could wash like Tubby as the water was very cold. Her father was very strict about wasting money and it was a waste of money to keep the fire alight overnight and somehow that made the hot water tap run cold in the morning. She decided not to bother about washing at all in the end, but she did brush her teeth. Tubby sat on the edge of the bath while she finished this daily nuisance.

Jean's mother was cleaning the grate ready to light the fire in the ideal boiler. Queenie Pearce was an attractive woman in her thirties; tall and slim with very dark brown hair, and green eyes.

Jean's father was already out and about doing farmer's chores. He had to start early; fetching the cows in to be milked and filling their horse's mangers with hay. The farm wasn't very large and consisted of the farmyard where lots of chickens roamed about; the two fields where the cows grazed and the piggery where the sow and her litter resided. Two other fields were used to grow fodder for the herd of shorthorns. They in their turn produced the milk that was sold locally. Jack and Frank Pearce ran the farm with the help of Matthew Bowen, a local man. Emily Pearce looked after the hens and sold the eggs from the old dairy which was attached to the farmhouse. The new dairy was very modern and scrupulously clean. The milk had to be pasteurized before Jack took it round to his customers in a cart pulled by Duke, the smaller cart horse. Dobbin, the larger horse was used for heavy farm work like ploughing the fields and pulling the heavy hay-cart.

"Have you washed?" asked Queenie.

"I cleaned my teeth," she replied earnestly.

Her mother stood up and studied the little girl. Her heart always melted at the sight of her child. Jean had been born after Queenie and Jack had been married for eight years. She and Jack had almost given up hope of ever having a baby. Jack would have liked a boy to carry on the family name and to help him run the farm one day, but Queenie was secretly pleased to have a little girl.

However today, this little girl was decidedly scruffy. Her fringe came down into her large blue eyes and she had toothpaste all around her little pink, defiant mouth. Queenie swept her up into her arms and swung her round and round laughing and cuddling her precious daughter.

"Look at you," she said holding Jean up to the mirror above the mantelpiece. Jean looked and laughed as well.

"Let me look at Grandma's dog picture," she begged.

Hanging beside the mirror was a picture frame containing a pipe-smoking dog. Queenie hated the picture, which was not at all to her taste really; but since her mother in law had given it to them for a wedding present, there it hung.

"Auntie Elsie is coming this afternoon remember, and you want to look nice don't you?"

"Why?" replied Jean.

"I want to be proud of you."

"Oh, all right. Can't I wash after breakfast?"

"No, run along and spend a penny and then have a nice wash, Jean. Breakfast won't be long. Oh and don't forget, after you've been to the toilet, please pull the chain."

Jean's heart jumped into her mouth. PULL THE CHAIN. She hated flushing the toilet for a very good reason. Jean washed the area of her face nearest to her nose and eyes and decided that the rest couldn't have got dirty over night. After spending a penny, she gazed down in to the bowl. She couldn't see the dreaded "Chainman" but she knew he was down there, waiting. Frank, her cousin, had told her all about the Chainman who lived under the water in the toilet. He could only get out when the chain was pulled by little girls and then he would chase them with his big sharp knife. Jean wished that Tubby was with her but he was still in the kitchen. She opened the door wide. She needed to escape quickly. Clutching the long chain with her left hand, she edged as near to the door as the length of the chain would allow. She took a deep breath. She had to get it right first time because sometimes when she pulled the chain, it didn't work properly. She was always too frightened to go back in case he was waiting. Jean yanked hard and at the same time let go of the chain and flew through the door slamming it hard behind her to make sure it closed. As she ran she placed her left hand high up behind her back to protect herself from the Chainman's knife. She flew along the passageway to the safety of the kitchen.

"I do wish you wouldn't slam the door that way, Jean and don't slide down the banister either, it's dangerous. You'll get killed one day."

Jean stared at her mother.

She must know about the chainman after all. He won't kill me though, so there, she thought. Frank had told her not to tell her parents about the chainman, as they had enough to worry about what with Hitler and everything.

It was still dark outside and Jean suddenly remembered that she had not closed the blackout curtain or turned off the light in her bedroom. If Hitler saw a chink of light through her bedroom window he would drop a bomb on the house without fail. Forgetting all about the dreaded Chainman, she fled back upstairs to turn off the light.

"I wish it was summer and then it wouldn't be dark in the morning and Hitler wouldn't see the lights in the house until late at night," she thought.

"That child," thought Queenie meanwhile. "I'll never understand what goes on inside her head."

She set a match to the fire and then went to prepare scrambled egg breakfasts for her family, thinking how lucky they were to have their own hens.

After breakfast Jean was in the orchard searching for eggs. The chickens often laid-away in strange places. Although they had large nest boxes in the hen coops, it seemed that they liked to lay their eggs elsewhere. The horse's manger was a favourite place; or under the hen-house itself. Sometimes they lay eggs out by the main road in the hedgerow. Once Frank had found fifteen eggs all in deep nest and the ones at the bottom had gone bad. Sometimes a hen would come marching proudly home with a clutch of cheeping baby chicks behind her. The chicks, tiny balls of fluff, looked so sweet. They were of various shades through pale sunny yellow to dark brown. The dark ones resembled the cockerel that lived with the hens and whose job was to wake Jean up at the crack of dawn every day.

So far she had found twelve eggs, white ones, brown ones, and several light brown with dark brown speckles. She took the eggs to the old farmhouse where her Grandmother would be waiting to wash them. Jean's Grandmother lived with Uncle Frank who was not married and they lived just down the track. Granny Pearce was over seventy years old and very small for a grown up, Jean always thought. In fact her cousin Frank was almost as tall as her already and he was only seven years old. Granny Pearce was a widow and always wore long black clothes, and her main job was to look after the eggs. Jean climbed up the steps to the egg pantry door with the eggs in the wicker basket. She was distracted by the sight of a beautiful caterpillar moving slowly along the door frame.

Jean put the egg basket down carefully. She reached up and picked the fluffy creature up in her little hand. As she closed her hand around it she could feel it all wriggly against her palm. She wanted to show her find to her Granny.

"Look what I've found!"

Her Grandmother turned around from the sink to look at the little girl,

"What have you got there?"

Jean approached and slowly and proudly began to open her tiny hand. Suddenly the most dreadful pain shot through her fingers and all over the palm of her hand. A dreadfully piercing scream filled the pantry. Jean stared at her hand, which had been holding the beautiful, furry caterpillar. All of the little hairs had come off the caterpillar's body and were embedded in her palm. Jean continued to shriek at the top of her lungs.

Queenie heard her screams and came running. She began to extract the tiny hairs from Jean's grubby little hand.

"Don't cry my little-love."

She tried to be gentle but the protective poison from the caterpillar had now caused the hand to swell and turn an angry red.

"I'll put calamine lotion on it and that will stop it hurting."

Jean stopped screaming. "Why did it do that to me?"

"The caterpillar was frightened."

Queenie bandaged the hand and calmed Jean down with the promise of something nice from the shops later when they went to meet Auntie Elsie from London.

"Heaven knows what I can buy for her though," she thought. There was only one sweet coupon left in her ration book. The grocer and his wife had no children and sometimes gave Jean their own sweet coupons.

"Try to keep that bandage clean, Jean," were her mother's parting words as the child marched off towards the cow shed.

Queenie did not like Jean going into the cow sheds in case the cows trampled her. Queenie had lived in a town for the first twenty-five years of her life, far and away removed from the sights, smells, and the sounds of cows. In fact she was downright frightened of cows. That may sound strange since she was a farmer's wife; but even after Queenie and Jack were married, Queenie had kept her job in the City. She had been a shorthand typist in a solicitor's office. It was shortly after her father-in-law's death in 1936 that Queenie had discovered that she was pregnant. It was a joy that after eight year's of marriage, a baby was on the way. Jean arrived after a difficult birth on All Saint's Day.

Since she could no longer go off to work in London, she settled down to being a farmer's wife.

It was certainly a very different kind of life for a London girl. However she managed pretty well all things considered.

Jean arrived at the empty cowshed and was swinging on the field gate watching her father hosing down the entrance. She loved to be near her Dad and was always ready to lend a hand with any of the farm chores. Sometimes she helped to fetch the cows but usually they were waiting by the gate; they knew when it was time to be milked somehow.

Jean led a solitary existence as there were no children near her age in the road where they lived. However, she was happy as the day was long.

Some days she peeked under hedgerows, searching for the magical red and white spotted toadstools where the fairies lived. Sometimes she explored in the woods, looking for rabbit warrens. Life was never dull in the country. Jean sometimes wished she went to school like Frank, her cousin who was eighteen months her senior.

As she swung on the gate, her dad would give it a push with the yard broom as he swept the mess away. Cows are not particularly clean in their habits. Later still, she made her way back to the dairy where George, the new farmhand, and her Granny were bottling the milk ready for the afternoon's milk round. Jean watched as the milk passed across the coolers, which were shiny silver-coloured metal grooves. The white milk trickled down just like a waterfall and then poured into a big shiny drum. From there it was poured into the bottles. She often helped in the dairy but today she couldn't because of her bandaged hand.

Somehow the once white bandage had changed to green and brown. Her Mum would not be very pleased. Just as she was wondering what to do next she heard her mother calling her. She wandered back through the orchard toward their whitewashed house.

"Bathroom!" said Queenie.

Jean scuttled off upstairs followed by Tubby who had been waiting by the ideal boiler for his young mistress to return. He didn't like the cowsheds. He was not very fond of the huge smelly creatures. Having made a gallant attempt to remove the morning's grime, the child went up to her bedroom to change into her best dress for the trip to Oxted. They were to meet Auntie Elsie's train. Queenie was waiting for Jean in her room. Although clothes were rationed, Jean did have some nice hand-me-downs which had once belonged to Christine Mathez. Queenie's best friend Ruth lived in Hendon. Ruth's husband Roly was a stockbroker and they had a daughter a little older than Jean. Roly still lived in Switzerland and occasionally parcels got through to Ruth, past the German blockade, to England. Sometimes Ruth sent gifts of Swiss chocolate to Queenie. This rare wartime treat was probably the most scrumptious taste that Jean had ever experienced, because sweets had been rationed ever since she could remember.

# The Bus-Ride

Jean dressed in the red frock, white ankle socks and white cardigan. They waited for Jack who would take them to the bus stop in the village by cart. The farm did own a little car but petrol was scarce. Duke, one of the farm horses pulled the milk cart every day delivering milk to the villagers of Holland and Limpsfield. He also had an afternoon round for his customers in Old Oxted.

Jack left them at the bus-stop to wait for the little green bus to arrive. Jean stood on the edge of the pavement to investigate a puddle. She stared into it whilst Queenie was talking to an old lady. Jean saw her own reflection in the dark water. She wondered how deep the water was and tentatively put her toe in to find out. As her shoe touched the dirty water, her mirrored face began to wave about and she laughed at her twisted reflection.

"Jean!" Her mother's angry voice made her jump. "Don't be so naughty. Can't you stay clean for five minutes?"

Jean looked at her wet shoe and put it behind her other leg to wipe the water off thus leaving a dirty wet mud- mark on her clean white sock.

"I give up," said her mother.

As Queenie bent down to clean the child up, the bus arrived and splashed through the puddle drenching them both.

Queenie paid the three penny bus fare to Oxted; Jean could ride free until her fifth birthday.

Jean wobbled as she walked down the aisle to the long back seat. She bus shook as it pulled away and Jean clung on to anything she could reach to keep her balance; grabbing other people's shoulders as she passed them by. Jean liked to kneel on the back seat and watch through the rear window. The drive to Oxted took twenty minutes. It was always interesting to travel on the bus. One trip was so exciting because the road between the War Memorial and the Haycutter Pub had been badly flooded. The little stream had burst its banks and the road was awash with deep water. The bus had crawled slowly through the flood setting up huge waves which lapped into the adjoining fields. It had been quite thrilling. Jean wondered if the bus had broken down, what would they have done?

Jean started to look around for bus tickets to add to her collection. She had loads already; of many and varied colours. She spotted a bright yellow one under the seat in front. A yellow ticket was rare and cost a florin. Frank didn't have one yet and Jean was determined to get it. She couldn't reach it so she got right down on the floor. She crawled under the seat to pick it up. It was bad luck that the bus went round the corner by the war memorial just then and Jean rolled across the floor. She returned triumphantly to her seat, brandishing the prized yellow bus ticket. Her nice white cardigan was smeared with the grey dust from the floor of the bus. Jean was quite oblivious of this and was thinking how envious her cousin Frank was going to be when she showed off the latest in her ticket collection.

They arrived in Oxted and went to the station to wait for the London train. Only one train per hour passed through Oxted; and none at all on Sundays.

The train was arriving; they heard the whistle blowing as the engine chuffed and puffed out of the tunnel. The Oxted tunnel was one of the longest in the land, they said, at over one mile in length. It carved through the chalk of the North Downs on the Southern Railway line from Victoria to Brighton. As the train came into sight Jean jumped up and down in excitement. The steam poured out of one funnel as the train driver tooted his whistle. This was accompanied by black smoke from the chimney on the top. With a terrible screeching and grinding the train halted beside the platform and the doors began to swing open. Queenie grabbed her little daughter just as she was about to be knocked over by the swinging doors.

Through the smoke Queenie spotted her old friend. Elsie looked very smart wearing a navy blue hat and a matching coat, Queenie couldn't help feeling a little dowdy. She hadn't had any new clothes since the outbreak of war in 1939.

It was a big jump down from the carriage to the platform for Peter.

Jean suddenly felt very, very shy and hung back behind a pillar that seemed to be holding the station roof up. She wrapped both arms around the wooden structure and clung to it while she waited for them all to alight from the train. She watched her mother and Elsie get the big pram out of the guard's van and put the little baby into it.

"All aboard!" cried the smart man in the navy uniform. "Stand clear."

Then with a grunt, a shudder, and a loud whistle the train began to move away. Jean wished that she was going too, because her lovely white cardigan had suddenly developed dirty grey streaks all over the front.

"How on earth did that happen?" she wondered.

There were a handful of Canadian soldiers returning from their leave in London to rejoin their units. One soldier approached Jean.

"Hi there, kid," he called out.

"Hello Uncle Alf," she called back. He was one of the soldiers who worked in the secret ammunition dump in the woods by her home. He was a frequent visitor to their house where he often helped Jack on the farm during his leave-time.

Alf was of Red Indian decent and extremely proud of the fact. He had been terribly homesick when he had first been stationed in England. Jean and Frank met him in the woods one day. They had wandered near to the camouflaged nissen huts containing all manner of weapons, including bombs. He had escorted the children home and stayed for tea. Since he had lived on a farm back in Canada, he had offered to help with the haymaking that year and had become a welcome visitor ever since. Frank and Jean would listen spellbound to the tales he told them about the Native Canadians on that distant continent that he called home.

Since the Brighton train did not stop at Hurst Green Halt, everyone who wanted to go to Holland, including Queenie's group, had to board a different train.

Alf helped Queenie, Elsie and the kids on board the stopping train to Uckfield via Hurst Green Halt and Edenbridge. This train only had three carriages and they had to make sure they got into the first coach because their station, Hurst Green Halt, was so small the other two coaches would not fit on to the platform.

Alf loaded the pram into the guard's van up front.

With a huge shudder the train pulled away. It was chugging forward with a series of jerks. Jean fell over with a plonk right in front of Peter who toppled over her to land sprawled out on the floor of the carriage. They both dissolved in laughter as they picked themselves up. Their mothers sighed in despair at the two children who now had matching dusty faces.

"Oh dear," said Queenie, "Why do I even bother to try? Jean can't keep clean for five minutes!"

"Peter's just as bad. You should see him when he gets home from school."

"Can we look out of the window, Mum?" Peter begged.

"May we," corrected Elsie, who was tending baby Wendy. "Isn't she a darling?"

"Yes she really is. I'm glad I had a girl this time."

The two women sat down on the grubby looking seats of the second-class carriage. They could not relax as the trip would take just eight minutes.

"At last you're here, I've missed having company these last years. How is it in London?"

"I can't tell you how awful it's been lately. Hitler seems to be determined to wipe London off the face of the earth."

"We hear the bombers going over nearly every night"

"It's the waiting that's the worst. First you hear the wailing of the sirens; and then the drone of the planes and the sounds of explosions. I take the children down to the underground station where we often stay all night. When we go up to the surface and head for home, we're all hoping that home is still there!"

"It must be terrible, especially without John there to help. How is he? Have you heard from him?"

"Not lately," said Elsie quietly. "All I know is that he's in North Africa."

"He'll be fine," Queenie tried to cheer her up. "While you are here, you'll have a nice rest."

"That's what I'm here for, peace and quiet in the countryside."

The children had managed to slide the window right down and were looking backwards along the train. The other carriages swayed along behind them.  Suddenly it went dark!

Jean and Peter turned their heads to find that the train had entered a short tunnel. In front they could see the little round hole of light ahead. The train was speeding towards this bright light. Jean opened her mouth to speak but the rushing wind tore the words from her mouth. All she could do was splutter and cough as the sooty air hit her in the face. As she pulled her head back inside the train, Peter got the full blast of smutty air. He also began to choke on the smoky fumes in the tunnel. They pushed the window up and sat down, completely unaware of the state of their faces.

"What on earth have you been up to?" asked the women in unison, staring at the two black faced youngsters.

"Nothing," they replied.

"I suppose there's no answer to that," said Elsie.

The little steam train pulled in to the tiny station. Heavy doors swung open and the passengers alighted. Queenie, Elsie carrying the baby struggled to get off the train. Alf helped Queenie retrieve the pram from the guards-van. Jean dragged Peter along the platform to watch the people who'd got into the wrong carriage. The second coach was situated under the railway bridge and all the people who wanted to get off had to clamber out on to the bank. They jumped down on to the embankment on the other side of the railway bridge. It was a precarious operation but the two children thought it was a huge joke. Finally the guard waved his flag.

"All aboard!" yelled the guard. "Stand back from the train."

With another big shudder and a great snort the little train leapt forward on the way to Edenbridge. Jean and Peter stood on the platform and waved until, with a few toots from the funnel, the steam engine and three little carriages chugged round the bend.

"That train goes right past the end of our second field," said Jean proudly, as though that mere fact made the train her own personal property.

"I'll take you there tomorrow," she whispered, pressing her forefinger to her lips; frowning secretively. Peter's eyes grew rounder in his head as he wondered what he was going to see the next day. When his Mum had said that they were going to the country, all his friends had told him he would be bored stiff but things were looking up. Jean was not like the little girls at his school either; for a start she was not exactly clean and tidy and that was a definite plus in his book.

The terrible two turned round and watched as the three grown ups heaved the pram up the wooden stairs that led from the platform to the road above. At last they were ready for the walk home to the farm. Alf rejoined the other soldiers and waved goodbye. A two mile walk was waiting for Queenie and company. Their journey wound through the tiny village of Holland.

Jean and Peter walked along behind their mums. It had been ages since Queenie had seen Elsie and they had lots to catch up on.

The village had three main shops.

Mr. Hopkins ran the shop where Queenie got most of her groceries. He winked at Queenie as he kindly gave the children some boiled sweets.

"We've got some nice bacon in today," he mentioned.

Queenie bought some gratefully.

Jean loved to watch the big, circular knife whizzing round as it carved off thin rashers. It seemed to be ringing as it swished through the large joint of bacon.

Florrie Stacey owned the Greengrocery at the top of the hill. She grew most of the vegetables herself out in the back allotment. There was always a funny smell of boiling beetroots in her shop. Next to Florrie's establishment was the Butcher's shop. There were dead animals hanging from hooks in the window, dripping blood. Jean did not like that shop. There was sawdust on the floor to absorb the blood and there was a nasty smell lingering in the air. Several carcasses hung from the fence outside along with dead pheasants. Outside the shop was a wrought iron bench where old men from the village sat there chatting. Many of them had been in the Great War of 14-18. Jack, the big, jolly faced butcher, was also the local bookie. Everyone knew that betting was illegal, but that had never stopped the locals from having a little flutter.

Further on was the little Post Office which also sold cigarettes, sweets and newspapers.

The little group turned into the road that led up over the railway line and connected the village to Red Lane. Queenie stopped to chat with her friend, Mrs Pinner, for a while.

Leaving the village Queenie and Elsie trudged up the hill and over the first bridge which crossed one railway line. The two little urchins followed on behind; their little cheeks bulging with gob-stoppers. These boiled sweets came in four different colours, red, orange, yellow and green. Jean liked green best and Peter preferred red which was a good thing because Jean had never had to share her sweets before. The sweets were so big that the children had to take them out of their mouths in order to speak.

"Don't run," said Elsie. "We don't want you choking."

Peter extracted his sweet to speak but it squirted out of his fingers, hit the side of the pram and bounced along the gravelly road. He scrambled after it and recovered the valuable item.

"Don't put that in your mouth............," began Elsie but she was too late.

Peter wiped it on his short trousers and shoved it quickly back into his mouth. Jean shot him an admiring glance. Parents had funny ideas about dirt on the ground. Didn't most food grow in the ground before you ate it?

They continued their journey, crossing a second railway bridge.

At last they reached home and the proverbial kettle had been put on for the much needed cup of tea. Peter and Jean had a glass of milk, fresh from the cow, which Peter rather enjoyed much to his surprise. By now he was feeling a bit sleepy after the long journey and after a special tea of dippy eggs and bread soldiers, followed by home made cake, the two children were packed off to bed.

A little later on, as dusk was creeping over the fields to envelop the farmhouse, the two women were sitting by the fire in the warm kitchen. Baby Wendy was feeding contentedly at her mother's breast. Across the valley on the opposite hills the setting sun had illuminated all the gothic windows of the stately Caxton Home for Printers and the nearby Sailor's Retirement Home. It really was a dazzling sight; and then suddenly it faded, and dusk finally swept over the valley. Queenie got up and closed the blackout curtains. Then she put on the electric light.

"I remember when you only had oil lamps," said Elsie.

"I forced Jack to get electricity installed. Mind you we still keep the lamps handy for when there's a power cut. Relax, Elsie while I check the blackout curtains upstairs."

Queenie peeked in at Peter who was fast asleep in the large feather bed he would share with his mother. Jean was curled up in her bed with Tubby nestling in the curve of her body, purring gently. The curtain was pulled tight and no chink of light could escape to attract the dreaded bomber planes of Hitler's Luftwaffe.

"Good girl," thought Queenie, pulling the covers up under Jean's chin. She gazed down at the sleeping child, and wondered what would happen to her if, heaven forbid, England lost the war and Hitler's S.S. arrived to take everything away from them. She pulled herself together and with a last look at her little angel, she stroked Tubby and made her way back to the kitchen. As the bedroom door closed, Tubby arose, and waited as Jean's sleepy eyes opened. She pulled the covers back and he crept into the warm bed. They snuggled close together.

This also, was the routine of the day.

# Trains and Bombs

The next morning, after breakfast, Jean took Peter with her to bring in the eggs. The normal farm chores still had to be completed even though they had visitors. With Peter to help it did not take as long as usual. Her Granny told Jean to show Peter around the farm and accompanied by Tubby, they scurried off.

The first animals Jean took him to see him were Duke and Dobbin, the huge carthorses in their stables. Jean crept in under their huge bellies but Peter hung back; a little scared of their huge feet. Tubby also hung back and washed himself whilst sitting on an old tree stump by the field gate. There were a lot of puddles in the yard after the heavy rain of the previous evening, which of course Tubby himself had predicted. Today he washed only his face and left the back of his ears alone.

Peter really enjoyed seeing the animals up close. They had a look at the sows and apart from the smells which Peter was unaccustomed to he was surprised at how clean the animals were.

"We did have piglets but they went to Mr Porter."

"Who's he?"

"The butcher; you saw his shop yesterday."

The children walked through the gate into the first field where the cows were eating the juicy grass and chewing the cud.

"They all have names, you know," said Jean proudly. "That big strawberry shorthorn is Beauty; she's the leader. Then there are Belle, Daisy, Primrose and Ruby," she named the whole herd and pointed them out.

"What do you want to do now?" Jean asked.

"Can we go and watch for the trains?"

"We may have a long wait."

Jean knew that the trains ran once an hour but as she didn't have a watch, she couldn't tell what time it was.

"Let's go then."

Off they went, squelching through every puddle in the field until they got to the second gate. The cows had churned up the mud by this gate. The two explorers squeezed through the middle bars of the five bar gate and set off across the wet grass heading toward the railway line.

Tubby sat on the top of the gatepost and watched them out of sight.

When they reached the row of tall trees that separated the two fields, Jean heard the sound of a train in the distance and broke into a run.

"Quickly," she yelled. "There's one coming."

Together they scampered towards the fence in the distance. It wasn't easy to run with their wellington boots caked in heavy mud. At last, puffing hard, they perched on the top rung of the fence that separated the field from the railway bank, just as the little steam train approached.

They excitedly waved their arms and shouted to the engine driver.

"Hallo, Hallo!"

The engineer waved back and smiled at the two muddy children and so did the passengers and the guard. The train passed under the bridge and with a toot, it chuffed out of sight. For a while they sat on the fence listening to the sounds of the train getting softer and softer and watching its smoky white billows in the distance.

"If you like we can wait for one coming the other way."

"When does it come by?"

"I'm not sure really. Let's walk along in the ditch to that signal."

They jumped on to the embankment and splashed through the water in the ditch, cleaning the mud off their boots as they waded. When they reached the signal they sat down on the wet grass and waited.

"Frank climbed up there," said Jean pointing up at the signal lever that stood like a signpost against the sky.

Jean indicated the metal rungs of the ladder leading up to a wooden platform where the red and white signal hung poised. Just then it gave a big clanking shudder and moved downwards.

"Oh good, that means the Edenbridge train is coming. Let's cross the line and watch for it."

Jean led Peter down on to the track. They could hear the train coming from down the line under the bridge.

"Be very careful and don't trip over."

"I don't want to be knocked down," said Peter hurrying.

They crossed the four metal railway lines and clambered up the opposite bank just in time. Suddenly the train was upon them.

This was no ordinary passenger train however. It was much longer and the engine was huge.

"It's a goods train," shouted Peter.

They watched in awe as the deafeningly noisy train passed. It had flat platforms instead of carriages. Each was covered with heavy camouflaged tarpaulins. Then followed; wonder upon wonders, two wagons carrying huge green, brown and khaki tanks.

Peter and Jean were so excited to see these war machines up close that they waved and shouted hysterically over the din.

"Ooh look!" shrieked Jean, pointing at the last part of the train.

"Soldiers!" cried Peter.

There were eight carriages full of soldiers on their way to London. Some of them waved back to the two children. They were dressed in khaki battle dress and they looked so smart with their cap badges gleaming. At the rear end of the train, low and behold, there was a second engine.

"That's funny. I've never seen a train with two engines before," said Jean.

"It must be in case they need to turn round and go the other way."

"In case they meet Hitler somewhere, I suppose," replied Jean. "Frank will be cross that he missed it."

They began to slide back down the railway bank to the track.

"Look how smooth these stones are."

"Let's collect some." Jean knelt down on the track. She couldn't resist collecting things. Anything that appealed to her had to be collected and hoarded away in her bedroom. She picked out some distinctive stones.

"I've found one with a sort of snail shape in it," she cried excitedly pocketing it.

They approached the signal, standing tall and erect like a soldier itself.

"Let's climb up," said Peter.

Jean was a bit scared but she didn't want Peter to know that. They began to climb up the rusty metal rungs. They were quite wide apart and it was difficult with her short legs in the heavy wellies. She wouldn't be outdone by a boy however and so she followed laboriously behind him. They reached the trapdoor. Holding on to the slats above, they dragged their little bodies through the hole and stood triumphantly on the platform just under the signal itself.

It was amazing how far they could see. The farmhouse was visible in the distance. Jean spotted her uncle walking across the field towards them. With him was Bobby the collie dog.

"Quick! We must get down. My uncle will see us and tell my mum."

They scrambled down the steep ladder and ran along in the ditch until they reached a copse. Emerging into the field they ran homeward waving at the man and the dog as they made their escape.

"That was lucky," said Jean, with a great sigh of relief.

"Why?"

"I'm not allowed to go near the railway line."

"We'd better keep quiet about the troop train then."

Tubby was waiting by the gate with a present for them.

"Look it's a vole" said Jean, picking up the wet, dead creature by the tail. "We'll give it a burial!"

"Why?" asked Peter.

"Cause its dead, stupid!" she retorted.

They dug a small hole under an apple tree and put the little vole in and covered it up again.

After the funeral, they both felt hungry and made their way to the kitchen. They squatted on the step and kicked off their muddy wellington-boots and went indoors.

"Good Lord! Look at the state of you. Where have you been to get into that state?"

Both children had wet backsides and clothes caked in mud.

"Nowhere," they replied in unison.

The two little "muckworms" were washed and changed and kept indoors for the rest of the day, which had turned chilly and damp. Jean's cousin Frank came over and she showed off her latest yellow bus ticket.

"I had two of them once," lied Frank, "but I swapped them at school."

Jean ignored this remark as she knew he was really seething with envy. In fact only last week he had been looking for one himself.

"We've seen something you haven't," she bragged.

"What?"

"A goods train carrying big guns and hundreds of tanks."

"And it had soldiers and everything," added Peter.

"I bet you didn't!"

"Did so!"

They went on talking about the train and the two boys got wrapped up in a discussion about tanks, guns and other things that boys seemed so interested in. Jean left them to it and went to find her stone. She washed it under the kitchen tap and took it to show her mother.

"Look what I've found Mummy," she said proudly.

"Oh darling, you are clever. That's a fossil." Queenie turned the stone over and studied it carefully. "What do you think Elsie?"

"I think you're right. Where did you find it, Jean?"

"Out near the edge of the second field," muttered Jean, trying not to lie but not to tell the truth exactly.

"I expect that it came up off the railway track then," said Queenie with a knowing smile.

"Could have, I s'pose," said a strangely fidgety Jean. She was standing with both arms wound around behind her, quite oblivious to the guilty appearance she conveyed to the adults who were trying not to laugh.

"I wouldn't like to think you'd been on the railway line; it's dangerous."

"Yes, Mummy, I mean no, Mummy."

"I've got eyes in the back of my head remember!"

Jean went back to join the boys and they played snakes and ladders until teatime.

This was not as easy as it should have been because Tubby kept insisting upon sitting in the middle of the board. That was only fair as they had placed the board right in front of his log fire, and on his mat.

Jack came back in time to join them all for tea and the children listened intently to the adults talking about Uncle John who was

23

somewhere in a desert with Monty. Jean was rather surprised about this because the old collie dog they had had before Bobby had been called Monty and she'd often wondered where he had gone.

"Uncle John must have taken our old dog with him."   She wondered why they needed dogs in the army.

"I've got to go out tonight. I'm on Home Guard duty."

Jean's heart leapt into her mouth. That could only mean that Hitler was coming again! Several times a week her father had to go down to the crossroads by the Plumbers Arms and guard Red Lane against an attack by Hitler and his army. Jean imagined that Hitler came over from Germany every night with his soldiers. He would come up the main road to get to London. It was her father's job to stand at the crossroads and stop Hitler going any further up either the main road or Red Lane. Jack always took his gun and he and Uncle Laurie would set off and not come home until almost morning.

"You send him packing, Daddy" she said in a tiny voice.

"Don't you worry little one, Hitler won't get past us!"

Feeling a little apprehensive Jean went back to the fire and cuddled Tubby.

Everything would be alright.

Jack and Laurie usually popped into the Plumbers Arms Public House during their shift on duty at the cross roads. They became excellent bar billiard players and played for the pub team for many years.

Later that night as she and Tubby lay in her warm, cosy bed she lay awake thinking about her poor Daddy out in the night firing his gun at Hitler. She could hear the muffled sounds in the distance. It sounded like thunder but when she had asked her mother about these noises; Queenie had told her that it was the sound of bombing over London.

Jean tossed and turned until finally she fell into a troubled sleep.

A few days later, Queenie and Elsie were out in the garden hanging the baby's nappies on the line, when they heard the sound of an aeroplane overhead. Biggin Hill aerodrome was only a few valleys further east, and they often heard planes; but this one sounded different. The children were indoors painting pictures. As the 'plane got closer Queenie realized that it was a bomber!!

Recently the German Luftwaffe had become increasingly daring. Daylight raids were frequent. The plane flew over very low and plainly visible to the women.

"That barrage balloon in the corner by the cowshed will never stop it," said Queenie.

"Where are the rest?" Elsie commented. "They usually fly in squadrons."

"It's probably a straggler; they get separated by the spitfires."

"I hope the fighter-planes get him."

Just as she spoke there was a terrible wailing noise. The air raid siren on top of the Kensitas Factory had started up. It was a sound to make your blood curdle!

"We've never been bombed here, Elsie, don't worry."

Elsie had gone as white as a sheet and had dropped the washing on the wet grass as she began to run on shaky legs towards the kitchen door. Queenie ran after her, trying to calm her down.

"It's too late for the dugout; go into the scullery."

Laurie and Jack had dug a bomb shelter in the clay bank dividing the two gardens. Inside were oil lamps, food and drink, two hammocks for the children and basic furniture. So far it had only ever been needed at night.

They arrived in the kitchen and Elsie snatched up the baby and grabbed Peter.

"Stay near to me." She was very agitated.

Peter however was quite excited and asked if he could go out and have a look.

"No," was the stern reply. "We left London to get away from all this."

Jean was sitting in front of the fire, munching a boiled sweet and clutching the sweet tin to her chest. She was not in the least worried about the plane but more concerned that her mother would notice that she had helped herself to the sweets. Queenie didn't notice. She was only concerned in calming down her friend who seemed to be on the verge of losing control.

"Elsie! Pull yourself together. I'm going to make a pot of tea."

Peter wondered why grown ups always had to drink tea whenever there was any danger. It was the same in London. During every trip to the underground station during an air raid, cups of tea appeared. It was quite extraordinary. He went over to the window to see what he could see; nothing, what a pity. However he could hear the aeroplane. No, it was more than one plane. He heard the higher pitched whine of the fighters chasing the bomber. Gosh this was something. He watched intently through the window.

It was probably only minutes later that the sound of a muffled explosion disturbed the usually tranquil village of Limpsfield. The Jackdaws in the oak tree behind the farmhouse flew up in the air. Their loud tchack, tchackertchacks drowned out by the explosions. The bomber was returning. Peter heard another explosion as another bomb fell somewhere in the vicinity.

"Good God! They are bombing us," cried Queenie.

"I knew it!" Elsie was in tears. She swept up baby Wendy, who was yelling mainly because she had been woken up, and took her into the scullery where she deposited the babe under the sink.

The thunderous sounds as bomb after bomb exploded shook the whole farmhouse and Jean, sitting cross legged on the kitchen floor began to bump up and down with the vibrations. The bombs seemed to be dropping all around them; the explosions were rocking the very foundations of the farmhouse. As the noise of the aeroplane got louder and louder, they saw a flash as one of the bombs landed and exploded in the field where the children had been walking earlier. Peter shouted in glee.

A mass of earth was flung into the air and when the dirt settled Peter saw that a huge hole had appeared.

"Look at that!" His excitement was short lived as his mother pulled him away from the window and to his annoyance pushed him under the big oak table.

Queenie snatched Jean up from the floor as she heard a strange rumbling noise sound on the staircase. They scrambled under the table, just as part of the wall tumbled down the stairs and the rubble came to rest exactly where Jean had been sitting moments before. Several more bombs fell in the woods and fields nearby and then it was quiet.

The jackdaws came back to roost only to fly up again as the sound of the all clear siren rent the air.

Queenie went outside to survey the damage. There were two huge craters, one in each field, within a hundred yards of the farmhouse. Doris's house had suffered most damage. The blast had lifted the roof up and the curtains had been blown out of the gap. The farmhouse itself had some damage to the upstairs ceiling as well as the disintegration of the asbestos wall on the staircase. A long crack had appeared from top to bottom in the kitchen wall, outside and inside.

"Let's count our blessings," said Queenie.

"Is it over?" asked Jean, clutching the forbidden sweet tin. "I hope the cows are all right."

"I think the Gerry plane either got away or has been shot down over Edenbridge. What a good job I moved you, Jean," replied Queenie, eying the rubble on the floor.

"That's one bomb load that won't get to London."

"That's true." Elsie was feeling better now. "I cannot believe that I put Wendy under your sink. Suppose it had fallen on her in the blast?"

"Well it didn't. I expect we could all do with-----------------"

"A cup of tea!" laughed Peter. He couldn't wait to tell all his friends back home about this adventure; and they had said he'd be bored stiff.

Shortly afterwards, Jack arrived home. He was quite out of breath. He'd hurried back to check on his family. Jack checked the house for damage and was dismayed.

"That damage to the outside wall will take some work. Maybe I'll get Alf Hunter to do it and extend your kitchen at the same time."

"That would be wonderful," Queenie was tearful now that the impact of the incident hit her.

He helped Queenie clear up the mess and sat down to tell them what had happened to him.

"I was down near the two bridges, delivering milk to Mrs. Harrison, when the first bomb fell. I heard the noise and felt the blast at the same time. It had fallen in the field just opposite. Funny thing was, the blast knocked me off my feet and threw me into the ditch right across the road." Jack wiped his forehead and then went on. "I think I was unconscious for a while. When I came round properly and got up, Duke had bolted, cart and all and was heading off down the road towards home. I knew I'd never catch him so I went back towards Mrs. Harrison's. Guess what? The milk crate was on the ground with not a single bottle broken!"

"Well, I never," said Queenie. "Why did that plane drop the bombs around here?"

"I imagine that the spitfires spotted him and he couldn't climb high enough with his load. He flew low in a circle and dropped the lot."

"Were there any direct hits?"

"I don't think so. I couldn't see any fires burning," Jack replied.

"I think we'll go back home. It seems to be safer in London." Elsie was still worried.

"Don't do that, Elsie?"

"Please Mum, let's stay. I love it here," begged Peter.

"I haven't even shown him the brickyard yet."

"We'll stay for a few days," said Elsie. However she was no longer convinced of the safety of the countryside. For all it's tranquility, it was really no safer here than anywhere else.

# Bomb Craters and Tree Climbing

The whole family walked across the fields to inspect the bomb craters. Jack led the way to the edge of the yawning hole that was at least twenty feet across, and around ten feet deep. The rich soil was scattered about the hole in a circular pile, rather like the rim around a volcano. It was a terrible sight and showed just how much damage the bomb could have done if it had fallen on the house. Peter edged towards the rim.

"Can I go down inside?" he begged.

"No, you can't," Jack said.

Jean was looking at all the rocks that had appeared in the mud. They were a mixture of smooth and jagged stones. She picked up an interestingly shaped one.

"That is a flint stone," said Jack." Before people found a way of making metal, they used stones like that as tools. The people were called Stone Age men."

Cousin Frank appeared on the other side of the pit, with his father.

"There's another crater in the next field," Frank yelled excitedly across the abyss. "There must be at least one in the wood; we heard some falling over that way."

"Can we go and see?" asked Jean. She could not bear it that Frank had seen more than her.

"Is it safe, Jack? There may be an unexploded bomb."

"We've had a good look round," Laurie replied.

"Off you go then."

The children were already galloping off. Running as fast as their short legs could carry them they headed towards the woods at the edge of the field. Sliding under the wooden fence, they began to weave their way through the thick bracken which was higher than Jean's head. She suddenly vanished from sight. The two boys ploughed their way through the giant fronds. Jean had found an easier way and was crawling on all fours between the hairy bracken stalks and thus she reached the bomb crater first. This one was even better than the one in the field because it had uprooted a huge oak tree when it fell. The once mighty tree was lying across the crater. The topmost branches rested on another tree about fifty feet away.

Jean clambered over the roots of this oak and climbed up on to the horizontal trunk. The gnarled bark of the trunk made a perfect foothold for her tiny feet. She crawled along the trunk towards the leafy branches that were resting on the other tree across the void. She climbed on without a trace of fear although by now she was ten feet off the ground. Just then the boys burst through the thick undergrowth in time to see the soles of her wellies disappearing into the foliage. They leapt forward to follow the little tomboy with whoops of delight. They had only traveled a little way, when to their dismay, Jack and Laurie appeared, having taken the more conventional route along the riding path.

"Oy! Come on down," Laurie shouted in his booming voice that must be obeyed.

"Where's Jean?" asked Jack.

Frank looked down at his boot and began cleaning the mud off one of them with the other. He was sure to get the blame as he was older and was expected to look after his cousin. Before he could answer however, a little voice from high up in the branches called out.

"Daddy, look at me!"

Jack looked towards the sound and to his horror, there was Jean's green face looking out from the foliage like the proverbial Cheshire cat. Her body was obscured by the leaves and her face had become smeared in the green lichen from the tree trunk when she had wiped her hair from her eyes.

"Stay where you are," he shouted. "I'm coming up for you."

"It's alright Daddy, I can get down easily."

As she spoke, her green face vanished. The leaves and the branches began shaking violently and two wellies appeared followed by a red skirt as the child began emerging backwards and slithering down the rough tree trunk as nimbly as a monkey. She descended the tree trunk that crossed the gaping bomb crater with agility. Her dad held his breath and the two boys looked on enviously. Then she was safely down again quite oblivious of the danger she had been in. After this the men marched them all home to the comparative safety of the farmhouse. The house was now in complete darkness because the blackout curtains had been drawn. Queenie had a warm drink ready for everyone. Queenie stared at Jean's clothes and above all, at her newly acquired green face.

"What ever happened to her face?" she accused Jack.

"Don't ask me," he chuckled.

"I think a bath is called for," she retorted.

For once Jack did not argue.

Tubby got up and stretched, and went towards the staircase. That was his cue for bed.

In bed, all warm and snug Jean made exciting plans for tomorrow. If she could manage to evade her parent's watchful eyes she and Peter would have a great time. Tubby curled up beside her and purred her to sleep.

The adults discussed the traumatic events of the day. Laurie had heard that the bomber had dropped twenty five bombs; all of which had fallen in a large circle in and around the Oxted area. Very little real damage had been done. Spitfires from Biggin Hill had succeeded in shooting the Nazi bomber down. The pilot had parachuted out and had been captured by the local Home Guard. He, the pilot was only twenty years of age.

"It's incredible that someone so young was flying a bomber," said Queenie.

"I don't expect that they have that many pilots left. We are all losing our fliers."

"By the time the war ends, if it ever does, there will be no young men left," whispered Elsie.

Queenie put her arm around her friend and tried to cheer her up.

"John will be alright I'm sure."

"He knows how to keep his head down," said Jack. "Don't you worry, old girl, he'll be back for Christmas."

"I pray that you are right."

As Jack got ready to go off for his stint at the crossroads between Limpsfield and Oxted, the women got ready for bed. Queenie placed the torch by the back door with some snacks in case there was an air raid during the night. She kissed Jack and went to bed.

Sure enough the siren wailed out the eerie warning at about two a.m. Every one woke with a start as the piercing siren wailed. Elsie couldn't believe her bad luck. It seemed that the war had followed her to the countryside. Peter was beside himself with excitement whereas Jean was worrying about Tubby who had leapt off the bed and vanished at the first sound of the siren.

"I'm not going without Tubby," she wailed, almost out-doing the siren itself.

Eventually the assorted party stumbled their way down the garden path to Laurie's dugout where they met up with Doris, and baby Joyce, Grandma Pearce and a highly delighted cousin Frank. They picked their way in the dark to the entrance of the mound and crept down the tunnel to the room under the ground that Laurie had dug for just such an emergency.

It was a very tight squeeze with the extra three but with two boys in one hammock and Jean and the two babies in the other, order prevailed. Doris put the tin kettle on the paraffin stove and before long everyone had a cup of tea, much to Peter's amusement. None of the children wanted to sleep, of course, except the babies. Grandma Pearce told them stories and Elsie kept alert to the sounds outside. After awhile the steady wail of the all-clear siren sounded out. It made a jubilant solo sound that cheered everyone up. The drowsy families made their way homeward. Peter felt quite let down as nothing remotely exciting had happened. Elsie was feeling decidedly better about it all. In London she would have been seeing signs of destruction all around with glowing fires and the acrid smell of smoke in the air. Maybe they were safer here after all.

They stumbled along until their eyes got used to the darkness. Beside the backdoor was a very disgruntled Tubby who had been shut out during the flurry of activity earlier. Just to show his annoyance when he came indoors, he deposited a very wet, very dead vole at Elsie's feet. This had a far more frightening effect on the woman than all the bombs in the world and she let out a fearsome scream where upon Tubby shot out of the room like a rocket and everyone fell about laughing.

"That's the end of a very scary day," said Elsie. "I'm really ready for bed now."

Queenie quickly flung out the offending vole and ushered the children back to their warm beds. Tubby was already on Jean's bed wondering why all the fuss.

Jean rubbed her eyes and gave Queenie a kiss.

"Good night, Mummy dear, see you tomorrow." She was asleep before her head hit the pillow. Tubby waited until the coast was clear and snuggled under the covers once more. The farmhouse was quiet at last, nursing the new crack in the wall. Looking back, that was the one and only time the war really affected the Pearce family.

# Jean discovers School Dinners

A year passed and still the war raged on the continent. Great Britain held off the might of Hitler's forces. Rationing made food and clothing scarce but the brave people survived. The British held on to their freedom as one after another the European nations were over run by the Dictator's troops. Jean had her fifth birthday in November and was due to go to school at the start of the next term. She should have started in the September but a bout of bronchitis prevented that. It took her a few weeks to shake off the nasty symptoms and the teachers decided that she should begin at the start of the next term.

The New Year dawned and Jean had started school.

"Hurry up and eat your porridge," said Queenie. Jean was always slow in the morning as she really didn't like going to school. Rosie Braysher was waiting to walk Jean and Frank to Merle Common. Rosie was fourteen and in her final year at the small Merle Common school.

"Ugh," said Rosie "How can you eat porridge?"

Jean liked porridge and eating it was performed in a special ritual. She would cut the cereal into squares which floated in the milk and then devour each piece with relish.

"It's nice," Jean told the older girl.

"I think it's horrible," said Rosie.

"That's enough Rosie! Don't put her off it." Queenie was cross. Food was so scarce the last thing she needed was for Jean to become fussy.

It was very cold that morning as the three children made their way along the road to the common where they took a short cut. The journey only took about twenty minutes and they were wrapped up warmly against the winter weather. Jean wore a brown woolly coat, a pair of sturdy Clark's shoes and a red pixie hood hat that prevented chilblains forming on her ears.

All the puddles had frozen solid during the night and the water at the "petrol pump" had frozen too. The Petrol Pump was in fact just a big metal tank which stood beside the road and was used to fill the army truck's water tanks. Queenie had christened the tank-the petrol pump and when the children were young. Doris would pretend to fill Joyce's pram up as if it was a motor car. Each evening soldiers congregated in the vicinity waiting to be picked up after their stint at the secret ammunition dumps deep in the woods and taken back to their billets. Frank held on to the edge of the metal rim and hoisted himself up to look inside.

He bashed the ice and decided it was thick enough to take his weight. Once on the surface he slid up and down on the ice calling out to Jean to have a go.

She didn't need asking twice and soon they were slithering on the ice together. Rosie reminded them that they'd be late for school and so they ran all the way there. Down the steep sloping hill they flew; getting muddy and wet. They arrived breathless and late at the school gates to see the last of the children filing inside. The children always lined up for roll call and then marched into the school building one class at a time.

"Bellingham!" boomed out the headmaster's voice. "You are late again."

They scuttled inside and hung up their coats on pegs in the cloakrooms.

Jean went into her classroom and got ticked off by Miss Huckle.

"Why were you late?" said the ogre.

"Please Miss, I fell over."

"That is obvious. You are covered in mud. Go and wash those shoes."

Jean fled to the cloakroom and spent twenty minutes trying to clean her shoes. She was in no hurry at all but Valerie Newman was sent to fetch her.

In class they were reciting poetry. Miss Huckle immediately pounced on Jean.

"Recite the poem you learned last week," she snarled.

To her teacher's amazement Jean was word perfect.

"All along the back-waters the back waters
Through the rushes tall
Ducks are a dabbling up tails all."

Jean recited the poem to the end without a single mistake.

"Alright sit down," said the ogre and Jean sank back into her chair and kept quiet as a mouse until dinner time.

At dinner time most of the children ate in the school canteen. This was a separate building. Unlike the red brick school, the canteen was a shack with a corrugated iron roof. Inside were long tables where the children would eat with the rest of their class. Today as Jean queued for her meal, she had a bad feeling that it was going to be mince! Not that she disliked mince but it always appeared with a mound of bright orange swede. Mashed swede! She could smell it before it arrived.

"Please Miss, I don't want any swede," said Jean.

"There are children in London starving" said the big fat dinner lady.

"They can have mine" Jean said, innocently.

"Don't answer me back!"

"I wasn't."

The dinner lady put a massive dollop of swede on Jean's plate. Jean stared at the enormous pile of steaming orange mash. She was never fussy at home, but at home she was never given swede. In fact school was the only place she had ever seen it. She slid into her seat next to Val.

"I'm not eating that!" she said furiously. "Look how much she's given me."

She ate everything else on her plate and moved the orange mountain to the edge. It looked even bigger. She mashed it flat with her fork but it then covered the whole plate. She put her knife and fork down. The dinner lady came back and saw the untouched swede.

"You'll eat that, young lady, or I'll tell Miss Huckle," retorted the fat dinner lady.

"I can't eat it. I'll be sick."

"I don't care if you are sick; you'll eat that swede," thundered the dinner lady.

"I won't!" said Jean in a small but determined voice.

"Oh yes you will or you won't get a pudding!"

"I don't want a pudding."

Miss Huckle arrived.

"She won't eat her swede," said the nasty dinner lady.

Miss Huckle frowned at Jean. "This child is always making trouble," she thought.

"You will sit there until that swede has gone," said the ogre.

"I'll be here for a long time then," muttered Jean.

"I'm going to give you the ruler for your insolence," snarled Miss Huckle.

"Hold out your hand."

Jean held her hand out and Miss Huckle seized it and rapped the thin edge of the ruler across Jean's knuckles. Jean tried hard not to cry but it hurt more than getting the cane.

"Now eat that swede."

Miss Huckle left the canteen.

Jean sat there, sullenly staring at the obnoxious orange stuff.

The other children ate their puddings and went out to play.

Jean sat there. Her knuckles were swelling and the pain was awful.

The whistle was blown for class.

Jean sat there.

The cook came out and told her to eat just a little bit but Jean refused.

The fat dinner lady tried to force some in the girl's mouth but Jean spat it out at her.

"I won't eat it and you can't make me!"

Jean sat there all through the afternoon lessons and during second playtime.

She could hear the others out in the playground and began to feel cross. That was when Jean made up her mind to run away.

When no one was watching, she crept outside and told Val to tell Frank she was going home. Creeping through the railings she set off at a trot over the common towards the comfort of home. When she reached the woods the air raid siren started up and she sat under a tree until the all clear sounded and then made her way slowly home. When she got to within sight of the farmhouse Jean decided to play in the wood until Frank arrived so that they would arrive home together and no questions asked.

She climbed up a beech tree that grew beside the petrol pump. The bare branches reached up to the sky and, from her perch up high, she could see for miles. The farmhouse lay beneath and to the left. In the distance she could see the ugly white Kensitas factory where cigarettes were made. It was a wonderful experience just like being in the rigging of a sailing ship; she remembered the story of Treasure Island. Her imagination ran wild and she imagined herself at sea with the wind blowing and the waves beneath her. She watched the occasional bird flying past and wished she could fly too. It must be marvelous to swoop around in the sky. The clouds were big and white and fluffy and seemed to take on weird shapes as they slowly wafted by. Sometimes they looked like giants. One cloud looked like an old man with a long beard and Jean wondered if it might be God.

After a while she saw Frank and Rosie approaching.

"Frank, I'm up here," she yelled, at the top of her voice.

Frank stopped and began to look but he couldn't see Jean anywhere.

"Up the beech tree," she yelled again.

Finally he spotted her and running towards the beech tree, began to climb up too. It didn't take long before he was just below her. Together they admired the view.

"Mr.McCarthy sent for me," he said. "He asked if I knew where you were."

"What else did he say?"

"That he's going to tell your dad."

"I'm in for it now. We'd better go home."

They started to climb down but although it had been easy to get up; it was a different matter trying to get down. Frank began to climb down the other side of the tree. He became stuck when his feet wouldn't reach the bough below. Jean was right behind him and neither child could go back up as the next branch was out of reach. Rosie ran to the farm and fetched Jean's mother. Queenie came and began to climb up, only to get into a panic herself; and then she was unable to move up or down either. Rosie went to fetch Auntie Doris and Matthew Bowen who brought a ladder.

Eventually Doris managed to rescue Queenie, who had never climbed a tree in her life before. After Queenie scrambled down, Doris helped Frank down. Jean was at last able to move, and with Frank out of her way, shinned down like a little monkey.

Not a word was spoken on the way home. Jean knew there would be no play that evening. She knew there was worse to come.

The next morning, she got ready for school as usual and no one said a word about the previous day's events. Jean pecked at her porridge, with no enthusiasm.

"What's the matter?" Queenie could see that Jean was unhappy.

"Nothing."

"Yes there is; tell me."

Suddenly everything tumbled out; about the ruler, the dinner lady and above all the swede!!

"You mean that you ran away from school because of the swede?"

"Yes, they kept me in all dinner time because I left it. Even if Miss Huckle hits me I won't eat it. My fingers couldn't hurt any more than they did yesterday."

"Show me," said Queenie.

Jean held out her hand and her knuckles were red, blue and swollen. Queenie was horrified.

"I'll kiss them better," she said putting the tiny hand up to her mouth. "I'll speak to Miss Huckle," she said.

"No please don't, she'll only take it out on me worse if you do." replied the terrified child.

"Alright," said Queenie, but she was determined to get to the bottom of it.

They were not late for school that morning.

At dinner time everyone trouped in to the canteen. Today it was sausages and mash. No swede but broad beans instead. The dinner ladies filled everybody's plate.

When it came to Jean's turn; without a word, the big, fat dinner lady slammed down a plate in front of her. It was the very plate of cold swede that Jean had left the day before. She stared at it. Some children laughed but Jean didn't make any attempt to eat.

Suddenly the canteen door opened and the headmaster came in. Behind him was Queenie Pearce.

Queenie swept over to her daughter and surveyed the plate of stale swede.

"Is this what my child is expected to eat? How dare you treat a child of five this way!" she retorted, Queenie picked up the

41

offending plate, took it to the door and flung the swede out into the playground. Then she took the empty plate to the hatch and put it down gently.

"There, it's gone," she said to the trembling, fat dinner lady.

As she left, Queenie winked at Jean.

Every child in the canteen looked on in utter amazement and admiration.

Two weeks later a new teacher arrived to teach the juniors. Miss Sharp was sweetness itself. The fat dinner lady disappeared shortly afterwards as well. No one knew why and no one cared. Life went on.

Jean soon became a celebrity at school, not because of the swede affair but because she discovered that she could walk on her hands.

"You should be in a circus," said Valerie.

"I will be one day," she said assuredly; but Jean had to ask her mother what a circus was.

A few weeks later she was in trouble again for being one of the dozen or so to be caught sliding on the ice. Some of the boys had been sliding in the playground where it sloped off towards the shed at the bottom. They had been told not to do this as it was dangerous; but it was also such fun. If you ran fast and launched yourself on to the slippery slope you could slide all the way to the bottom. The children caught sliding were summoned to the headmaster's office.

Each child was asked if they had been sliding on the ice. They all denied it but got the cane for lying anyway.

"Did you slide on the ice?" asked the headmaster.

"No, someone pushed me on to it," Jean told a lie.

"Hold out your hand," he said.

Swish went the cane. It didn't hurt much on her palms. She had covered them in soap as Frank suggested. He had not been caught.

Jean told her mum that night, hoping for sympathy.

"It serves you right. It was dangerous and you could have hurt yourself. Rules are rules; someone might have fallen over on that slippery ice," admonished Queenie.

Jean went to her room with Tubby and sulked until supper time.

On the whole Jean enjoyed school, especially reading and writing and composition. She had a marvelous imagination. Sometimes they would listen to the school's radio broadcasts. Her favourite was one about a man who told them about life on Earth before humans had arrived. Once he pretended to be in a jungle full of all kinds of prehistoric animals. He heard a noise in the undergrowth and suddenly he was running for his life; the dinosaur was chasing him. Jean was captivated by this tale and could see it vividly in her imagination.

She hated sums and although she could add up and take away, do division and even multiplication the rest was always totally beyond her. When reciting her tables she often just opened and shut her mouth silently.

One day a rounders ball went missing and as no one owned up to losing it, all the people who had been playing with it the day before were asked to go and search for it. It remained lost. Miss Webster told them all to look for it at home in case they had taken it home with them. Jean told her mother, who was very angry and once more turned up at school and demanded an apology for calling her daughter a thief. Miss Webster said that she had meant the remark for the one who had taken it, not necessarily Jean herself.

"I am sure it was not Jean who took the ball," said Miss Webster.

Queenie was a very quiet woman and she did not swear or shout as some of the mothers did but she was always ready to defend her child.

The children were called to the hall one day.

I have something important to tell you all," said Mr McCarthy. "If you see anything unusual lying on the ground, you must never pick it up."

He explained that German planes might drop bombs disguised as tins or boxes.

From then on Jean led a quiet school life and got on well.

# Holidays, Fun and Cows.

The Easter holidays arrived and that year it was exceptionally warm. Jack took Frank and Jean along to the Triangle; a quiet part of the River Eden. He had a funny black swimsuit which, Queenie said, came out of the ark. It went up over his chest and had straps over the shoulders.

"It also has the moth," Queenie mentioned.

Uncle Laurie had shorts to swim in. Jack taught Jean to swim in the muddy waters where the cows came down to drink; by a little sandy beach on a bend. The river there was wide enough to splash, paddle and swim about in safely. Jack swam away towards the tunnel that went underneath the railway line. The field was contained by high banks on each side where two railway lines intersected. The area was triangular in shape. Jack swam on into the tunnel and out of sight. Jean waited on the edge of the bank until he came back.

"Take me with you."

"It's dark in there and deep."

"Take me piggy back," she insisted.

He let her climb on his back and swum away from the bank.

Jean clung tightly on to his straps with her hands and gripped on tight with her knees. It got darker and darker but she wasn't frightened at all because her Dad would look out for her; he was a

Home Guard! A deep, rumbling noise echoed in her ears but Jack swam on valiantly.

"It's just a train on the line overhead," he panted.

"I know that!" she replied.

When they got to the other end of the tunnel, Jack hoisted her up on to a brick wall where the water thundered over into the river below.

"This is the weir. It's really deep this side of the weir," he said. "You must never swim here."

The water poured over the top like a small waterfall.

"Watch me," said Jack and then he jumped up in the air and turned right over and entered the water head first.

Jean watched in amazement as her father disappeared through the hole that his hands had made. The last bits of him she saw were his toes as he vanished into the water with just a little splash to show where he had gone. She watched, but he had vanished. The water was green and murky. For what seemed the longest time, she saw no sign of her Dad. Then suddenly, his head popped up yards away from where he had disappeared. Jean had never seen anyone perform a dive before.

"How did you get over there?" she called out across the water.

Jack flicked his blonde hair back out of his face and swam lazily back towards her.

"I'll teach you to dive when you can swim properly."

"I can swim."

"When you can swim further than you can now, I mean," he promised." Jump on we'd better go back."

Back in the pool where Frank and Laurie had been waiting, there was excitement because a fisherman had caught a pike. They all went over to see the prize specimen. It was really big and had teeth, Frank said. Jean wondered if it had any relations still in the water and curled her toes up in case.

After a picnic and another swim they made their way home. Jean and Frank were perched on the crossbars of their father's bikes. It had been a lovely day. Jack didn't get much time off as the farm kept him busy every day of the week.

Jean had been invited to Nova Heaysman's birthday party which was to take place the following Saturday. Clad in her best dress and looking neat for once, Jean accompanied her mother to Nova's home in Holland village. Jack gave them a lift over there but they would have to walk back.

To begin with, she enjoyed the party. There was cake, jelly and sandwiches. Then they played musical chairs.

Gradually Jean became aware of a little girl called Mavis Tully who was speaking to Jean's mother. Then this girl climbed into Jean's own mother's lap. Jean stood stock still in horror. She was experiencing her first feelings of jealousy. No one except baby Joyce had ever sat on her mum's lap and she didn't like it one little bit. Jean went over and pushed Mavis roughly.

"Jean, that's naughty," said Queenie sharply.

Mavis smirked. All Jean could think was that her Mum must love Mavis Tully more than her and she ran into the kitchen crying. She was so upset that she went out of the back door and set off for home. When she reached the "Diamond" Public House, she ran along a little muddy path and climbed the style and then jumped on to the stepping stones that crossed a stream. With tears streaming, she ran across the field towards the stile that adjoined the level crossing on the railway line. When she reached the stile there were a dozen or more young bullocks grazing there. Jean walked in amongst them with no fear but as she climbed on to the stile, she remembered how frightened her mother was of cows and decided to wait for her.

About twenty minutes later, along came Queenie picking her way across the field in her dainty high heels. Queenie always wore high heeled shoes if she was going out. She always looked elegant. Making her way through the cow-pats she suddenly came face to face with a "Cow" and stopped dead in her tracks. Queenie was frozen to the spot. What should she do? Go back or go on?

"Hello Mummy. I waited for you."

"Thank goodness, there you are. Don't move! Stay still and they may not attack us." Queenie still couldn't move but was worried about Jean being attacked and trampled. The animals took very little notice of either of the people; they were busy chewing the cud.

"It's alright mummy," called Jean reassuringly. "They won't hurt you. I just walked right through them."

Jean jumped down and marched back right through the group of animals who stood head and shoulders above the little mite, just to prove her point.

"Watch out! Those cows will toss you," called out a terrified Queenie.

"Don't be silly, Mummy, they aren't cows they're BULLOCKS!"

Queenie nearly passed out. "Oh my God we'll all be gored to death," she thought.

Suddenly a tiny warm hand pressed into hers and the five year old calmly led her terrified mother away from the peaceful "beasts".

"Mummy, they won't hurt us. They are only babies; just baby boy cows. Frank says they are being bred for the army. I didn't know that animals went to war. First Monty our old dog went to Africa with Uncle John, and now these bullocks are going too."

"Oh Jean, you are funny," said her mother, feeling much better as they circled the animals who took absolutely no notice of them. "One day I'll explain all about that."

From the safety of the stile, she looked down at the creatures, seeing them in a different light.

"Poor things, its corned beef for you I'm afraid," she thought as they hurried home.

At the fireside that evening, Jean sat quietly wondering about Mavis Tulley.

"Do you love me, Mummy?"

"Of course I do; more than all the tea in china!"

"More than you love Mavis Tully?"

"Is that what upset you? Mavis was sitting on my lap because her own mother is in hospital having a baby and Mavis was feeling lonely." Queenie gave Jean a big hug.

Jean felt a lot better. She changed the subject.

"Don't you think that cows have got beautiful eyes?"

"Have they? I've never got close enough to see."

"Yes they have the longest lashes and look so kind and gentle."

"I think we must be looking at quite different animals." The lady from London laughed.

Queenie remembered that Doris, who had grown up on the farm and knew all the cows by name, had once been tossed by a cow. Doris had been trying to help a calf get free from some wire when the calf's mother had come up behind and tossed poor Doris into the air with her horns. That had done the animals no good in Queenie's eyes.

On Sunday Jean went with her Dad to fetch the cows for milking. They collected some early mushrooms.

"Why is Mummy frightened of cows, Daddy?"

"She's just not used to them pet."

They ate the delicious mushrooms with home-cured bacon and eggs. Jack left on his milk round and Jean went to do her chores. Frank came too and they split up, each searching for nests of chickens laying-away. Frank went along the side of the road and up the hill, whilst Jean decided to look along the path leading to the clay pit. The clay pit was one of her favourite places. It was where the men from the brickyard dug the clay out of the hillside and took it to the brickyard to make bricks. In places; high up the "cliff face", the tree roots dangled out into space. Some roots were thick and up to ten feet long. They waved about loosely having been uprooted and Jean thought they looked like the elephants trunks she'd seen in her books. Jean and Frank would climb up the clay bank and swing from these roots. Sometimes they would crawl to the cliff edge above and shin down the roots and then swing out into space using the long roots like ropes. Their parents knew nothing about these dangerous games of course. Jean mooched along looking for eggs when suddenly a strange boy leapt out in front of her. She had never seen him before.

"What are you doing?" he demanded.

"I'm looking for eggs," she replied, thinking what a funny way he had of speaking.

"Where do you live?" she asked.

He didn't answer. He was a bit taller than Jean and very scruffy. His clothes were much too big for him.

"I know where there is a bird's nest," he said. "I'll show you. Come on."

Jean followed him. He stopped and pointed at a very large grey metal tank in a thicket.

"In there!"

"I can't see in there. It's too high."

"I'll help you up."

He lifted her up to the top of the old water tank and she looked down through a round hole on the top of it.

"You'll have to climb right inside to see the nest," said the boy.

It was a tight fit but Jean squeezed down inside the tank and squatted there.

"I can't see a nest," she began to say, when suddenly it went dark. She could hear the boy laughing and reached up but he had put some sort of plank across the hole and she was stuck inside.

Jean was furious and began to yell and thump on the inside of the tank. It made a strange booming sound. She wondered if anyone would find her or would she starve to death inside. She was already hungry.

Eventually Frank found her and she scrambled out covered in cobwebs and absolutely seething with anger. When Frank heard about the strange boy, he realized that it must be one of the evacuees from London. They lived with old Mrs. Reed and went to Limpsfield School.

The two children set off to find the culprit and that didn't take long. He was swinging on a gate by the brickyard cottages. Jean pointed.

"That's him!"

Frank strode to the gate and seized the boy. They both fell to the ground kicking and punching each other. Jean aimed a few kicks but managed to fall over instead. The noise brought Mrs. Reed and her grown up sons running out. The men separated the mass of arms and legs and dragged the two boys apart.

"What's all this about?" asked Douglas Reed.

"He shut my cousin in a tank!" shouted Frank. "I'm going to teach him a lesson. You don't treat girls that way."

"Looks more like a boy," sneered the boy.

"Tommy, you say you're sorry," said Mrs. Reed.

The boy made a noise that might have been an apology.

"Tommy is unhappy here; it's hard for him being taken away from home and carted off to live with strangers," said Cecil, Mrs Reed's other son.

"Perhaps you could all be friends?" said Mrs. Reed.

"We're going now," said Frank with a snort.

They ran towards home. On their arrival, Queenie asked what Frank had done to his nose.

"I fell over," was the standard reply.

"Thanks," said Jean as Frank left. "Do you really think he thought I was a boy?"

"I expect so; you act like one." Jean was secretly pleased as she'd always wished she had been a boy. She knew that her dad had wanted a boy.

Of course the children's escapade was discovered. Mrs. Reed telephoned Frank's mother. Queenie explained to the children what it meant to be a refugee. She told them that Peter could have been one if his home had been bombed. Jean said nothing because she knew that Tommy would never be a friend of theirs. War had been declared and he had started it.

The next time they saw him, he was swinging Frank's cat, Mickey, around by the tail. This time it was Jean who attacked Tommy. She flew at him with arms and legs flailing and he soon dropped the frightened animal and he and the cat whizzed off in different directions. Jean looked everywhere for Mickey but he had gone off into the woods.

By teatime Mickey had not returned. The children searched the woods calling Mickey, but still he didn't come home. Frank went to bed without him. The next day he was still missing but the children had to go to school. After school they rushed home to look for the little ginger and white cat but were met at the petrol pump by Queenie and Doris. They both looked really upset and as gently as possible, told the children that Mickey had been found dead. Apparently he had got caught in a rabbit snare. Frank held back his tears as best he could and ran home alone. Jean burst into floods of tears.

"It was all Tommy's fault," she blurted out, through her sobs. "I hate him!"

Time softened the blow and Frank was given another kitten a few weeks later. Mrs Addison, who lived in Red Lane, told Doris that her cat had had kittens and Frank could choose one for himself.

The children traipsed down to Mrs Addison's house where another friend of theirs lived. Her name was Bubbles Addison and she was a little older than they were. There were several people visiting the kittens and one was a little girl of Jean's age called Ann and with her was an older boy called Lionel and through the next few weeks they became friends with Frank and Jean. These children did not attend Merle Common School and they had never met before. Ann and Jean were to become close friends.

Frank chose a ginger and white kitten that reminded him of Mickey.

His mother said that Mickey was probably the kitten's father and the "son" part stuck. Jean asked why Tubby wasn't the father and her mother said that Tubby had been neutered. Jean hadn't a clue what she meant but didn't argue. Son of Mickey became the kitten's name. Two weeks later Tubby went missing for a day and Jean was frightened that he was dead too. He came back in a sad state with a rabbit snare around his tummy. Luckily he had managed to get one front foot through the snare and being a very strong cat had uprooted the whole thing and limped home. He convalesced for a couple of weeks, revelling in the attention.

"Cat's have nine lives," said Queenie.

"Do they? How many do people have?"

"It's just a saying," said Queenie. "Tubby will be fine."

Jean had seen dead voles and birds but Mickey's death affected her deeply. She didn't like it. It was permanent and Mickey was gone forever.

About this time, two more children moved into the neighbourhood. They came to live at Copperbeeches with Mrs Rhoder, their Grandmother. They had unusual names; Averil and Desmond Ould. They attended Merle Common School and often Jean walked home with them and when that happened Averil and Desmond usually managed to get grubby. Their mother did not like them to run wild but they often managed to come up to the farm and play.

Averil belonged to Jean's gang. The other members were her friend Valerie and little two year old Joyce. Later two more girls joined; Pauline and Jeannie Russell who came to live in the brickyard cottages. The gang was called the Silviney Club and Jean made up all the rules! Tests had to be performed from jumping across the shallow river to climbing up the big beech tree and hanging off a high branch and letting go. The drop was about ten feet and quite daunting to everyone but Jean. Of course Joyce couldn't do anything and they let her sit and play with her doll. Jack found some tough rope in the barn and fashioned a swing suspended from the lowest branch of the beech. No end of fun was to be enjoyed by all. The ropes were very long and the swing swung across an area of fifteen feet. Jean and Frank would get the swing going so high and then would let go of the ropes and eject themselves into space. They fly through the air to land tumbling amongst the bushes. This was all hilarious fun; they could sit on the wooden seat or stand upright to get the swing flying higher and higher. Frank could even climb hand over hand up the ropes to the branch above. The trunk of the beech, which had to be several hundred years old, had toe holes carved in it; probably by some child many years previously. This enabled Jean to climb up into the hollow where the tree had at one time split into two trunks. There was always some smelly water trapped in this hollow. There were three beeches all within thirty yards of each other. Each tree had had initials carved in the trunks many years before. Spaced between the beeches were three ancient yew trees; also hundreds of year old. Now the six ancient trees together with many young birches, willows, tall hollies and towering ash trees sheltered Jean's house from the roadway beyond.

The headquarters of the Silviney Club was in the copse on the side of the hill. The copse was concealed from the road by a very old yew tree. Under the dark hanging branches were two dew-ponds. The deepest one was lower down the hillside and was always full with water. It was black and smelly water and the children had to walk around it holding on to branches to prevent themselves from falling in. The other dew-pond had dried up years ago and it was their secret place. Here the children scooped out the old dead yew tree needles and dug into the side of the hill to create an earthen sitting area. In the centre they would light a fire and bake potatoes in the ashes. Jean dug out a secret hollow amongst the roots of the yew and hid an old biscuit tin there. This tin contained the names of the gang members and the rules.

The school holidays passed by happily and Desmond would go off with Frank and their friends leaving the girls to get up to their own games. Frank killed a snake in the brickyard which he said was an adder. He baked it on the fire but no one really wanted to eat it.

"Cowboys eat snakes," he told them, but even that did not entice anyone to try it.

Sometimes Frank and Joyce went to visit Laurie's Dad who lived in Hurst Green on Knights Hill.

Frank's cousin Gillian Perryman and her friend Sheila Baldwin would be there and the children would play games on the Green near the Railway Station. Sometimes during the summer several children would play rounders together. Just nearby was a large building called Saint Agatha's Hall where the locals held meetings, jumble sales or even went Olde Time Dancing. It was also the Girl Guide's meeting place. Doris was a Brown Owl and she and Freda Luff taught the guides different skills. Jean was too young at the time but determined to be a Girl Guide one day.

# Something terrible happens.

The weeks passed and soon the summer holidays were upon them. The endless summer days stretched out before them and although part of each day involved work on the farm, these were enjoyable chores. The rest of the daylight hours could be spent playing in the clay pit and climbing trees in the woods between home and Edenbridge. Exploring the neighbourhood was an adventure. These children would be gone for hours at a time; travelling overland to the outskirts of the little Roman town of Edenbridge, just six miles away as the crow flies.

One sunny morning, soon after a hearty breakfast, Jack was delivering milk in the village as usual. As the morning passed, he began to feel unwell. He had to carry on with his deliveries as people were waiting for their milk. He had developed a headache and it got worse. Suddenly everything went dark. He fell to the ground almost unconscious. He tried to crawl back to the horse and cart but he couldn't manage it; the pain in his head was so bad and he couldn't see.

Several people saw him and one lady said later that she had thought he must be drunk.

One of Jack's loyal customers could tell something was dreadfully wrong and she fetched Mr. Hopkins; one of the few people with a car. Mr Hopkins drove Jack to the farm in his grocery van. Queenie was horror struck. Between them she and the grocer put Jack to bed telephoned Dr. Cohen.

Dr. Cohen examined Jack; who was drifting in and out of consciousness, but was unable to diagnose the cause of Jack's blindness.

"What did he have to eat today?"

"We all had eggs and bacon and mushrooms."

"Where did the mushrooms come from?"

"Jean picked them in the meadow," said Queenie.

Doctor Cohen pronounced toadstool poisoning for want of a better cause. The truth was that the Doctor had no idea why Jack was blind.

"I can't move my legs," Jack said before he drifted into semi-consciousness.

Jean sat on the stairs listening. She was very frightened.

"Will he die?" she asked her Auntie.

"Of course he won't."

"Why can't he see us?"

"I don't know. Were the mushrooms like the usual ones?"

"Yes. I had them too. Will I go blind?"

"I had mushrooms as well," said Queenie. "I'm sure it is something else. I want a second opinion."

"They think he ate a toadstool by mistake," she told the young doctor who came by the next day.

"Could he have?"

"No he didn't. They were just the normal mushrooms!"

That doctor left and told Queenie not to worry, but of course she was worried out of her mind. Jean was terribly quiet. If her Dad had been poisoned, it was her fault.

Three days later Jack had lapsed into a coma and a specialist was called.

"He's had a stroke," said the new Doctor.

"He is only forty two," said Queenie.

"It may be what we call an embolism; a blood clot that explodes in the brain. He could have had a weakness there all his life. The clot burst a capillary and that would account for the blindness and paralysis."

"Will he recover?" asked Queenie.

"Time will tell. He needs lots of rest. You will have to try to feed him liquids. I'll be back tomorrow."

The doctor left and Queenie sat down on the floor beside Jean and they clung to each other.

It was six long months before Jack was fit and strong again. For two months he could not see or speak but grim determination on his part pulled him through. It was a bad time for them all. Jean slept with her mother during this time and Queenie even let Tubby sleep in their bed.

Uncle Frank took over the deliveries of the milk and a farmhand was hired temporarily. That left very little money for the two families to live on.

Jean was left to her own devices and explored far and wide. She became an adept tree climber and climbed so high up the beech tree that she could see the chalk pits the other side of Oxted. She had absolutely no sense of danger.

One day she and Frank were up in the largest beech tree, swinging from the lowest branches and then dropping down to the ground. Jean decided to climb along a branch even higher up. She sat astride this great branch and travelled along far away from the trunk

"Go on; drop from there," Frank dared her.

Jean lent forward and holding on with both hands, she swung her legs down. She hung there for ages, it was such a long drop that she just couldn't let go. She had a funny feeling in her chest which could be described as panic. Eventually her hands slipped off the lichen covered bough and she plummeted down to the ground. She fell on her back and got the wind knocked out of her. Since she did not answer when Frank spoke, he thought she was dead and ran home to fetch his mother.

Jean came round and picked herself up. Seeing that Frank had gone she mooched off to her house and went in to the kitchen to sneak something to eat.

Meanwhile Frank and Doris arrived back to where Jean had been lying. When they discovered that the little girl had gone. Frank began to cry.

"I told you she was dead! Now she's gone to heaven."

He sat down and shook as he wiped the tears away.

"Don't be silly," said his Mum. "I expect she went home."

After that incident, Jean was told not to climb trees; of course she took no notice.

By Autumn Jack was well enough to go back to work and life returned to normal.

Harvest had to be gathered in and with the help of Matthew, Alf, George and Uncle Frank, haymaking began. The whole operation would take several days as they had no mechanical help. The children pitched in too; running hither and thither bringing in loose hay that had been dropped and throwing it on to the hay wagon. There were three fields of hay to be harvested. The hay had been cut, dried and made into stooks which were standing upright, looking like small wig-wams.

This particular evening, they had almost finished bringing in the hay from the furthest field. Uncle Frank noticed ominous clouds in the darkening sky and decided that they needed to get the final load in before the storm.

"We'll lose it if it gets wet," he told them.

Hay must be dry when stacked. If it was stacked wet, it would go mouldy or even worse, if stacked wet there could be internal combustion. Some farmers used the new method of baling the hay using a combine-harvester. Most farmers could not afford the new fangled machinery. If a farmer lost a haystack through fire, it meant he would have to buy winter fodder for the cattle and horses. Frank and Jack could ill afford that expense. The hay had to be brought in that very night before the rain came.

The children were only too happy to stay up. Queenie brought out drinks of precious lemon and barley for the hot dusty workers. By then it was practically dark even though they were on double summer time. Off they set with Duke pulling the smaller hay cart and Dobbin drawing the large wagon. Frank and Jean sat on the back of the empty wagon swinging their legs over the tailgate. The ground was very rough and bumpy and they kept being thrown up in the air as the wheels hit ruts. This made it all the more fun and the children dissolved into fits of giggles. Doris kept a wary eye on them in case they should be tossed off altogether. Working in the half light, the troop of workers picked up the sheaves from the ground with pitchforks and tossed it on to the two carts where Frank and Alf stacked it carefully. Overhead a sudden crack of thunder made the children jump.

"I didn't even see the lightening," Frank yelled.

There is nothing as spectacular as a summer storm.

"It's quite far away but you can bet it's coming our way," shouted Uncle Frank.

"Load on as much as you can," he yelled. "This will be the last trip tonight."

At last the two carts were full to overflowing. Each one was piled higher than any of the previous loads.

"We'll have to go very slowly all the way back."

"Can we ride on top?" Jean was rubbing her eyes.

"Jump up on Duke's cart," said Doris.

Alf helped heave the dusty children up on top of the load of fresh sweet hay. He took Duke's bridle and they set off on the return journey. Dobbin led the way and the smaller horse followed. The big loads lurched from side to side as the carts rumbled over the uneven fields. The children loved this part of haymaking. It made up for the hard work, just riding up on top off the load. As they swayed to and fro, it was like being on a ship on the ocean. Every time they hit a bump they slid about on the shiny bundles of hay. There was nothing to hold on to except each other and they were laughing fit to bust for most of the journey. They came within sight of the farm and the carts passed through the gate into the Home Field.

Their cart began to lurch about even more because this field was set on a slope and one pair of wheels were a good bit lower than the other two. They travelled on very slowly as the rain began to fall lightly. Doris and Uncle Frank were with the big wagon and had almost reached the yard gate when the rain began to fall in earnest. What mattered most was to get the hay under cover; they could stack it the next day.

Just at the moment when Dobbin was going through the gate there was an enormous flash of forked lightning, followed by a loud thunder crack. At the same moment, Duke's cart hit a rut.

The load shifted to one side and the children felt themselves slipping gently downwards as the load slipped uncontrollably off the wagon. They were thrown to the ground and the hay-load fell on top of them. They were completely submerged in the hay.

Everyone came running to rescue the little mites from their dangerous predicament, but they struggled to the surface, completely safe and laughing their heads off. The next job was to reload the hay on to the cart which took ages in the drizzle. Their task was completed. Duke and Dobbin were put in their stalls and fed. The adults spent most of the night in the barn tossing the hay to get it dry enough to stack. When Jean reached the warm farmhouse her mother gave a cup of cocoa with two spoons of precious sugar. The dusty little girl had pieces of hay sticking out of her blonde hair. Jean was as brown as a berry with a smattering of little freckles on her nose. Queenie told her to have a strip-wash before going to bed. Jean went into the bathroom where she stripped and washed her hands. She and the faithful Tubby fell into bed.

Jean dreamed strange dreams in which she was able to fly like "Peter Pan." In her dreams she could bounce off the ground and into the air and then she could soar like a bird. Over the tops of the trees she would fly. She flew the way her father swam; only she swam through the clouds just like a swallow. It was a wonderful dream.

Sometimes when she had climbed to the high branches in her favourite beech tree she imagined herself flying with the birds. She wondered what it would be like if the air beneath her was really an ocean and speculated what it would be like to swim in that vast blueness. Jean had a wonderful imagination as is often the case with an only child.

# Jean dislikes her new teacher.

Autumn arrived and school began. There was a wonderful cupboard at the far end of the school hall. Inside were incredible things. The doors were made of polished pine with inset brass handles. Sometimes they were allowed to play with the wonderful "pre-war" toys that lived in the cupboard. There were coloured building bricks with pictures on, puzzles, dolls, stuffed animals, wooden toys, spinning tops. England was a country deprived of toys because of the war. On certain days Jean's class could use the tins of powder paints which were in the Aladdin's cave of a cupboard. They painted upon large pieces of grey paper. The paints had a funny sort of smell. Jean always managed to get paint all over her. In class the three "R's" were all important. Jean found reading very easy as her mother had been reading to her since she was tiny. Queenie had given Jean several books as birthday or Christmas presents. Jean's writing was barely legible, but her spelling was good. It was arithmetic that stumped her. She could never get her seven times table right and eight and nine times tables were a mystery to her. Why people needed to know tables at all was beyond her. Her new teacher was called Miss Webster, and she was strict but fair.

It was during this term that Jean became smitten by an older boy who joined their school. She thought he was beautiful.

His name was Robin Wells and he had incredibly golden-red wavy hair; he was fourteen.

"Do you love him?" asked Val. "I bet you do!"

Jean didn't really understand what Val meant. Valerie kept teasing her about the new boy all the week.

"You should write him a note."

"Why?"

"To tell him you love him, silly. I wrote a note to Brian Charman."

"Did you?"

That evening Jean wrote a note in her best writing,

"dere robin wells. I love you from jean pearce."

She put the note into her pocket.

In lessons she passed the note to Val.

Miss Webster swung round from the blackboard.

"What are you whispering about Valerie Newman?"

"Nothing, Miss Webster," Val and Jean both jumped out of their skins. The note fell on the floor between them, and Miss Webster walked over and picked it up and read it.

"Come to the front of the class, Jean."

Jean was very scared as she stood at the front of the class.

"Did you write this note?"

"No, Miss Webster."

"You signed it. Read it out loud!" she commanded.

"I can't read it," muttered the child, thoroughly humiliated.

"READ IT OUT LOUD", thundered the teacher.

"No."

Miss Webster left the room and returned with poor Robin who wondered what ever he had done.

"Jean has a letter for you," said Miss Webster. "Read the letter, Jean."

Jean stood still and stared at the parquet floor. She remained silent.

Miss Webster handed the note to Robin and told him to read it out loud.

Robin did as he was told and his face turned bright red as he did so.

As he read, Jean wished the floor would open up and swallow her. She was as pale as he was red.

"Now Jean, did you write this?" Miss Webster asked her once more.

"No, Miss."

"I saw you take it out of your pocket! How did it get in there?"

"My Mum must have written it and put it there."

The desperate child said the first thing that came into her head.

"Go back to your chair and write a hundred times, "I must not tell lies."

Jean fled back to her seat wondering if she could run away at playtime. One thing for sure, she did not like her new teacher and learned very little that term.

The incident set her back a great deal. She became shy and withdrawn. She did not like boys, her teacher, or her lessons any more.

She helped out on the farm and was happiest at home.

One Saturday afternoon, when everyone had gone shopping, Jean was alone with her Grandma. They were in the orchard when they heard a low, unhappy bellow coming from the cowshed. It was Beauty, the leader of the cow-herd. She was about to calve. The pair went in to check on her and to Jean's utter amazement she witnessed the cow actually giving birth in the stall. Jean had had no idea of where baby animals came from up until that moment.

Old Emily Pearce and Jean stayed with Beauty until the calf was able to stand on its wobbly long legs. Straight away the gangly newcomer to the farm went straight to Beauty's teats and began to suckle. Jean was thrilled to see nature at its best; a new life beginning.

Beauty's calf was special to Jean, and she was allowed to name it.

"I'll call her Susan," she said.

Susan was a strawberry and white shorthorn. The two colours merged and her hide seemed to be a delicate pink hue in places. Jean was given the job of looking after the calf when she was separated from her mother. Calves were always taken from their mothers. The cow re-joined the milking herd. All cows were expected to give birth each year in order to produce milk permanently. This milk was eventually sold to the local villagers and that was what dairy farming was all about.

Jean taught Susan to suckle milk from a bucket. It was a wonderful moment when the calf sucked her fingers as Jean drew the calf's mouth into the bucket of milk.

Jean grew remarkably fond of Susan, much to Tubby's disgust. One evening he brought Jean a present. Jean and her Dad were playing dominoes, when they heard Tubby meowing strangely outside.

"What's up with the cat?" asked Queenie.

"I think he's hurt," cried Jean.

"I think he's caught something." Jack knew that miaow.

Jean opened the door and Tubby sauntered in. The reason for the strange sound issuing from his mouth was simple; his mouth was full. It was full of fluff. He went up to Jean and deposited the fluff at her feet. She bent down to touch it.

"Mind it doesn't bite," Queenie said nervously.

As Jean bent down to look at this little fluffy thing she saw it move. She looked more closely and noticed two large brown eyes staring back at her. She gently lifted the tiny creature.

"Look Mummy, it's a baby rabbit."

"So it is!"

Jack inspected the little bunny-rabbit.

"It's not injured."

"Can I keep it? I'll call it Bambi."

"I'll have to make a cage and an enclosure for it," chuckled Jack.

That night Bambi slept in a shoe box by the ideal boiler in the kitchen much to Tubby's annoyance. He had brought it back to please Jean and he had probably expected her to eat it. Otherwise he would have eaten it himself. Thus a new member of the family came to live at the farm.

It was one more creature for Tubby to share his mistress with. Over the next couple of days Tubby turned up with two more baby bunnies. These were presented to Frank and Joyce and were given the names; Whiskers and Thumper. Jack knocked up a wire run for Bambi and a large cast-iron water tank became his home in the back garden. As Bambi matured he began thumping with his back legs, as rabbits do. The eerie sound boomed out across the garden at odd intervals throughout the day and night.

# A Touch of the Measles.

The government had resolutely decided that to save civilian lives, every home in the country was to be provided with an Anderson Shelter. These shelters would protect the people from the falling masonry caused by the bombing. Each night tons of shells packed with explosive material rained down over all parts of the country; dropped by the relentless German Luftwaffe. The damage caused was not just the annihilation of the houses, factories and other establishments where the bombs landed but the damage from the blast and the falling shrapnel had an equally disastrous effect. People were being killed and maimed due to this constant bombardment.

The Anderson and Morrison shelters had heavy duty steel plates as a roof, and the walls were of an extra thick steel mesh. Jack erected theirs in his bedroom and then put his rosewood double bed on top of it. Inside the shelter Queenie made up a soft bed for them to use when there was a raid. From then on, when the air raid siren sounded, Jean would run and climb in with her Mother, under the protection of the shelter. Jack slept on the top in his own bed. Queenie called him stubborn. The bed was so close to the ceiling that Jean wondered why he didn't hit his head.

The damp dug-out became obsolete. The children played there sometimes until it caved in during a storm. Then it became out of bounds.

Italian prisoners of war arrived to help the Canadian soldiers who worked with the loading and un-loading of the ammunition which was stored in Staffhurst Wood.

"That's a funny set-up; do you trust the enemy with our ammunition?" Jack asked Alf.

"They are okay," replied the Canadian using the American slang. "I guess they surrendered anyhow. Most of the Italians here are glad to be out of the war. I don't think your average Italian guy wanted to join with Hitler's bunch in the first place."

"Well I think they're a funny lot, those I-ties."

The Italians were very friendly and often stopped to chat to the children in "broken" English. One young Italian made Jean a tablet of clay with an emblem of an aeroplane stamped upon it. He painted the tablet of clay purple. She treasured this clay masterpiece. Another prisoner was good at carving and made her a wooden doll. All in all, life was very peaceful in Oxted, even though England was a country still gripped by the terrible war.

Frank was too busy with his own friends to play with Jean nowadays and Joyce was too busy playing with her doll Molly. On Jean's birthday Queenie gave her a doll of her own which she didn't really want. Dolls were for girls!

"Give her a name," said Queenie.

"Molly," said Jean picking the same name as Joyce's doll.

Queenie was a little disappointed with the girl's disinterested reaction to the gift.

Jean had been hoping for a bow and arrow set. Uncle Alf had told her stories about his ancestors who had been warriors. They had fought the British and the French with bows and arrows as recently as the late eighteen hundreds; less than seventy years ago.

Alf made her a bow and some arrows out of hazel branches. Molly disappeared into a cupboard in Jean's bedroom. Queenie was disappointed and Jean remained a tomboy.

Skipping was the latest craze at school. The longer that the rope was the better the game. One girl at each end would swing the rope into a huge loop. Then other girls could run into and out of this loop and skip for a while before exiting. The game was called Vote, Vote, Vote, and as the girls inside the loop skipped they called for other girls to enter. The trick was to jump into the loop and skip over the turning rope for awhile before leaving again without causing the rhythm to break.

Jack gave Jean a long rope from the farm store and she took it proudly to school.

She and Val had been playing a skipping game with some younger girls when the older girls joined in and then took over.

"You can't play with us; you're too small," one of the big girls told Jean and Val.

"Alright," said Jean, snatching back the rope. "It's my rope though."

She ran off leaving the older girl looking stupid.

There were lots of playground games. They played skipping, tag, and leapfrog and an involved game of hide and seek called tin-can-kettle. This game involved throwing an old tin can and while one person had to fetch the can back to the middle of the playground, all the others ran off to hide.

The game of five-stones became Jean's favourite past-time. Jean was really good at it.

At the bottom of the playground was a play-shed. The roof was held up by two metal poles, painted orange. Jean would run the length of the playground and launch herself upwards to grab the top of a pole and swing herself out to her full length whilst clutching this pole. She swung round and round gradually getting lower until she reached the ground. She was able to jump extremely high. At home, at the edge of the garden by the wood, were some tall, slender hazel saplings. Jean could climb hand over hand into these pliant trees until her weight bent them down to ground level. Then she would leap up and down holding on to the tree. She spent ages bouncing up and down on the grassy lawn. This strengthened her legs and ankles and formed her natural spring; which was of use to her in the future as an athlete in the British team, but that's another story.

After listening to Uncle Alf's stories about his "Red Indian" ancestors, Jean invented an imaginary horse and pretended to gallop everywhere on it. She very rarely walked normally. She was always being told to sit properly because she liked to tuck one leg underneath her. She then leaned sideways on her desk to write.

"You'll grow up with a twisted spine," said her teachers, but it didn't happen; she had a strong back.

As she grew older she preferred to wear plimsolls instead of shoes. Even during winter, she would wear wellies and take her beloved plimsoles to change into.

"You'll have bad feet when you grow up," said her teachers, but it didn't happen either; she had good strong feet.

School was just an annoying interruption to Jean's daily life.

One morning, to Queenie's dismay she noticed that Jean's face was covered in spots. On inspection the spots were not just on her face but everywhere.

"I think you've caught something. You had better stay home today."

Dr Walker arrived, as old doctor Cohen had retired.

"Measles," he confirmed. "Put her to bed in a darkened room and don't let her scratch those spots. No visitors, she's infectious," he said, sweeping out of the room and leaving poor Jean wondering what "infectious" meant and how she had got it overnight.

"Try to sleep darling," said her mother, who knew that measles could have nasty side affects.

"But I'm starving," whined Jean, who didn't feel very ill.

Queenie returned later with a bowl of porridge. In the afternoon, Jack came up to see her.

"Never mind, my little soldier," he said gently.

During her illness, Jean became delirious and imagined soldiers coming out of the walls and marching around her bedroom. Her mother kept painting her with pink stuff and made her wear gloves in bed. Most of the children in the village caught the measles and soon Frank and Joyce had it too. Frank apparently blamed her and was angry as he couldn't go to cubs. Queenie spent a lot of time reading to Jean, and the blackout curtains remained closed all day. A week passed before the red blotches disappeared and Jean was allowed out of her room. She went to see her cousins.

"Keep saying that you don't feel well and we'll get longer off school," said Frank.

"Mummy," whimpered Jean later. "I don't feel well again. Can I go back to bed?"

Her worried mother tucked the child up in bed again. Jean wanted Queenie to read to her; play cards, etc, etc, and soon Queenie saw through the ruse.

"You can't pull the wool over my eyes," she said with a chuckle.

Jean looked about but couldn't see any wool anywhere.

"Mum's going mad," she thought.

The next week, she returned to school. June Blackett hadn't caught measles and was the leader in the playground. Everyone did as she said, and Jean did too. June was brilliant at netball and played shooter. She was left-handed. Jean tried to copy her and be left handed but the netball went off at a tangent and hit Anna Pitman on the ear.

"You can't play anymore," shouted the bigger girls. Jean galloped off on her imaginary horse. She didn't care at all.

Jean spent a lot of time alone at home too. Frank was allowed to go over to the village to play with his pals and Jean wasn't invited.

There were lots of things to do around the farm and she had her cat and her rabbit to play with not to mention Susan who followed her about. Bambi very quickly grew to adulthood and began to make a series of great escapes. Jack had built him an enclosure attached to his water-tank home. Bambi dug tunnels under the ground that came up outside the enclosure. He would disappear for ages only to come back later when he was hungry. The food that his adopted family provided was unavailable elsewhere. He soon discovered that the breakfast cereal and carrots that Jean gave him did not grow wild. Jean worried that something nasty would happen to her little rabbit. At first, the entire family would be roped in to capture Bambi when he made his escapes. Fruitless hours were spent chasing the elusive little rabbit. He could twist and turn so quickly that it was impossible to catch him.

"He ought to be called Quicksilver," said a breathless Queenie, after one Bambi catching session. He had eluded the whole crowd of them in the fields. Finally they discovered him back in his run, eating a carrot as though nothing had happened.

# The Nativity Play.

Christmas was approaching and at school they were making cards. The teachers delved into the school cupboard bringing out wonderful paper chains and paper lanterns. Many children had never seen these things before and it was so exciting to help the teachers festoon the classrooms. Miss Webster related the nativity story. Jean and Frank went to Sunday-school at a little church set in the wood; St. Sylvans. The vicar intended to present a nativity play. Frank was to be a shepherd and Jean was cast as the Angel Gabriel. Brian Charman and Graham Ashford were in the cast too, doubling as Joseph, Shepherds and Wise men. Joyce had the important part of Child Narrator.

Jean practiced her lines laboriously. Queenie made her a halo out of silver paper and cardboard and sewed a long white robe for the costume, using an old sheet.

Just before Christmas, all the parents came to see the performance. Queenie had helped Jean learn the angel's lines and Jean was very confident. Queenie was not; she had stage fright instead of Jean.

When it was her turn to perform, Jean strode on stage and gave Mary the glad tidings.

"Hail thou that art highly favoured. Blessed art thou among women. For unto you a child shall be born and thou shalt call his name Jesus," recited Jean.

She then remained standing in the background with her arms across her chest.

"So far so good," breathed her anxious mother to Jack.

The play progressed and Jean appeared to the shepherds; still word perfect.

When all the participants were gathered around the crib, Jean had to stand up on a box behind them all to give her final speech. This also went perfectly.

Jean stood on her box with her hands folded across her chest. She looked so sweet; until her nose began to run.

To Queenie's dismay, Jean pulled up her long white robes and extracted a hanky from her navy-blue knicker-leg. She blew her nose loudly like a trumpet. Completely oblivious of the audience's smiles, she pulled up the robes once more and put the hanky back up her knicker leg again. Then she folded her arms demurely across her chest once more. Somehow her silver halo had slipped over to one side. The lopsided angel stood there to the end of the scene and several people giggled but it only made it more endearing really. Queenie was embarrassed at first, but then when people said, "How sweet," she felt proud.

Jean however was never allowed to forget about it. Auntie Doris reminded her every Christmas until Jean had children of her own, and then Doris told them; producing the photograph of Jean and her crooked halo.

On Christmas morning, Jean was awake very, very early. Of course it was still pitch dark outside but Jean was sure that Father Christmas had been. She crawled down to the end of the bed to feel for her pillow case. She never had a stocking for her presents it was always a pillow case. Jean's mother always managed to fill a pillow case with goodies each Christmas. Even though everything was in short supply, Queenie managed to find lots of gifts for Jean. Queenie was inventive and made toys. She knitted well and would unravel her own jumpers to re-knit the wool for her daughter. She knitted a pink rabbit and a nice cardigan which had exquisite embroidery on the front pockets. Some boiled sweets and a bar of Swiss chocolate which had been sent by Auntie Ruth. Jack gave her a wooden box of watercolour paints and two brushes. Some hair ribbons and an Enid Blyton book were also in the pillowcase. Jean gathered all her wonderful presents up and returned them to the pillow case and then went back to sleep. In the morning she would open them all over again.

The whole family gathered at Grandma Pearce's for Christmas Dinner. Uncle Frank had provided a chicken for the meal. This was a once a year treat, even though they lived on a farm, chickens were not killed for eating. The children did not recognize the young cockerel in his new guise, which was a good thing. After the meal, the children gathered round the roaring log fire and compared presents. Frank had a sheath knife that Jean would have loved. Joyce had another doll with eyes that closed.

Uncle Frank arrived with a pretty girl called Gladys. They were going to be married. She had wonderful dark hair that was a mass of curls. Grandma Pearce was wearing her jet beads. Jean was fascinated by them. They looked like black glass and the sides of the beads were cut into a mass of flat square edges so that they caught the light and gleamed and winked darkly in the firelight. The grown ups were drinking sherry and the children were allowed last year's elderberry wine, watered down. Auntie Gladys had got the silver three penny bit out of the pudding and was flicking it up and down in her fingers and Jean noticed the ring glittering on her finger. Her mother also had a ring on her finger. They were both shining and flashing fiery lights and Jean couldn't take her eyes off them.

"I want a ring like that when I grow up," she exclaimed suddenly.

"When you are fourteen, you can have my mother's ruby ring," said Queenie.

"Can't I have it now?"

"No, you're too young to wear a ring."

"Let me see it," begged Jean.

Queenie was wearing the old Victorian ring which had been her mother's engagement ring. It was made of gold with a central blood red ruby with two smaller rubies on each side. In between were two pairs of tiny chip diamonds.

"That is pretty," said Jean.

"At last you are interested in something feminine," whispered Queenie.

The families played games around the table. Ludo and Happy Families and then they played, "Murder in the Dark," accompanied by shrieks and screams. A game of "Sardines" followed to round the evening off. The children were struggling to stay awake. Grandma Pearce popped them all into her bed.

The adults sat around the fire and chatted and smoked their cigarettes and drank their glasses of sherry and almost believed that life was normal again. It seemed such a long time since they had lived normally; free of the threat of invasion and bombing.

"Churchill will see us through," said Jack.

"He's a war monger," replied his mother.

"Whatever he is, he'll keep Hitler off our shores."

"What a brilliant idea it was to put telegraph poles all along the coastline. The Hun must think they are big guns."

"It's given us a bit of time to prepare for an invasion," said Laurie. He was a staunch conservative and admired Winston Churchill.

The women talked of nicer things like the old days and the cinema and fashion. They were trivial things maybe, but it helped them to take their minds off the war. To think there was a future for England which did not include Hitler was the only thing to keep them all sane. Great Britain had not been invaded since 1066 and things would stay that way if the Oxted and Limpsfield Home Guard had their way.

# Doodlebugs and Foxes.

It was the season of Spring-time. School went on and on, boring day after boring day. Jean spent hours labouring over her sums to no avail as the mysteries of mathematics were quite beyond her. She enjoyed every other lesson however, especially Geography. Life went on and still the British held on to their independence. In fact things began to swing in favour of the Allies. America had entered the war, mainly because their base in Hawaii, a group of islands that no one had heard of before, had been bombed by the Japanese.

As the year passed, Hitler had another surprise for Britain; a dastardly new weapon. The dreaded Doodlebug appeared in the skies. This awesome flying bomb was propelled towards London from across the channel. It was a pilot-less aircraft, set to fly as far as London where-upon its engine would stop suddenly and the vehicle, loaded with explosives, would hurtle to earth. In an eerie silence it would crash and explode as it hit the ground. It was named V1; V for victory the Germans hoped.

Later still the German's invented another flying bomb which was so fast people called it a rocket. This was called the V2. These were dreadful machines but at least they didn't shoot back. The fighter-planes were able to shoot them down but it was not easy to intercept them because the Flying Bombs were so very fast.

Jean spent a lot of time alone now, playing with Susan, now a heifer, Tubby and Bambi. She lived in a world of her own and rode her imaginary horse everywhere. Uncle Alf had been transferred; probably to fight on the Continent but of course no one was ever told where the Canadians had gone. Everyone on the farm all missed him and prayed that he wouldn't be killed. The last time Jean saw him, he was walking into the trees at the bottom of Pollards Hill as he waved goodbye for the last time. They never saw or heard of him again.

It was a particularly cold winter that year; quite deep snow had fallen and Laurie made a sledge for Frank. Jack knocked up one for Jean but hers was rather heavy. They dragged their new sledges up to Merle Common and joined with the other local children in sleighing down the steep slopes. It was really good fun. Jean's fingers were numb with cold and when she got home, and into the warm kitchen, the feeling began to come back. It was so painful that she cried.

"Why do my fingers hurt now?"

"It's the blood flowing back into them," explained Queenie. "I hope you don't get chilblains."

"What are they?" said Jean, horrified at the thought of yet another ailment.

"We won't worry about that now. Go and fetch the sweet tin."

Jean sucked a nice big green sweet and forgot about the pain and just remembered the exciting feeling of whizzing down the slopes in the snow.

The cold snap had another effect on the residents of Connerton Farm. The foxes went after the chickens. At least two of their hens had been eaten; the tell-tale feathers in the orchard gave the game away. The hens were always shut away each night and the wily fox would wait until they were let out each morning before stealing his breakfast chicken.

One morning soon after seven o'clock, Jack came bursting into the kitchen. He grabbed his shot-gun from above the door and hastily loaded it. Jack had three guns; a double-barreled shot gun and two Point 22 rifles. He rushed off towards the barn.

"We've cornered that darned fox in the barn," he called.

Jean was dying to follow him but Queenie held her back.

They heard the report of the gun and waited for Jack to return.

When he came back his arm was dripping blood.

"You haven't shot yourself have you?" Queenie took his arm to look. There were nasty jagged bite marks on his wrist.

"I got him with the first shot and he fell so I went to pick the old beggar up and he wasn't dead at all. He bit me pretty hard and I dare not let go. I had to strangle him."

Jack needed stitches in his wrist. The outcome was that Queenie had a very nice fox-fur to wear.

Jean was intrigued by this garment because it had a fox's face at one end and a bushy tail at the other. Queenie didn't wear it often and it lived in her wardrobe for over sixty years.

During the Easter holidays, Jean was expected to play with Joyce. Joyce always brought Molly with her. Joyce was not allowed to get dirty which made life very difficult for Jean as everything she liked to do involved getting dirty one way or another. Before long however the problem was solved! Joyce could be deposited in a camp amongst the bracken in the woods. Jean tied her loosely to a tree with a piece of washing line. Then Jean could gallop off to play knowing that Joyce was safe and happy with her dolls. This went on for most of the Easter Holidays until one day Jean arrived home without poor Joyce.

"Where's Joyce?" demanded Doris.

Jean stopped dead in her tracks.

"She's on her way. I'll go back for her".

She spun on her heels and galloped off to the camp. Joyce was patiently waiting.

"I have come to rescue you, Princess," cried Jean. "Quickly we're late for tea." Joyce much preferred playing with her Molly in the safety of the bracken thicket. Jean made the camp special. There was a hearth made of stones. Sometimes she boiled water on a fire and they drank leaf tea. Potatoes were baked in the ashes. Both children were happy and the Mothers were satisfied.

Jean had invented another playmate. Although invisible to others, she pretended to have a huge Sugar Mouse which took the place of a horse. She imagined that she could ride on its back and be carried everywhere, high up off the ground. Being made of sugar it would be nice to eat as well. She told Joyce that sugar mouse was made of sweets and bananas and chocolate. No one could see him but Jean. He was very real to her though. Queenie began to wonder if Jean's vivid imagination was normal, and whenever this little niggling worry crept into her mind she just shook her head and hoped the child would grow out of it.

"It comes of being an only child," she told herself.

Queenie was busy getting ready for some special visitors. Jack's relations were coming to tea. His cousin Copeland Borlace was bringing Great Uncle Ned to visit. Jean had not met these people and was rather intrigued.

"Copland's a funny name. Is he a cousin like Frank?" she asked.

"It's a Cornish name, like Daddy's name. Your father's second name is Trelawney. Frank's other name is Courtney."

"Is my other name Cornish?"

"No, you were named Rose after me and Mary after both of your Grandmas."

"I see. Tell me again about Nana Thatcher."

"Help me with the washing first."

Queenie and Jean were in the scullery where the old copper bubbled away emitting a strange smell. The water had come to the boil and the clothes were bubbling and gurgling in the soapy water.

Queenie kept prodding them with the slimy yellow copper stick; trying to stir the clothes about.

"Can I do that?"

"No, my little love, it is very heavy work and your little hands aren't strong enough to stir the washing."

"Then tell me about Grandma Thatcher."

"My mother was the nicest, kindest person in the whole world and she would have loved you to bits if she could have met you. She lived in New Eltham and she chose me as her little girl when my real mother gave me away. She thought I was the best little girl in the world."

"Was she very old?"

"Quite old, that's why Jesus wanted her to live in Heaven with him."

"Will Grandma Pearce be going there?"

"Not yet, I hope darling."

"Will I meet my other Grandma one day?"

"I expect so; but not yet."

Queenie hoisted the washing out of the copper. There was an art to this and very deftly she swung the washing up and over to the sink where it was put through the wringer once to remove the soapy water. Then it was rinsed several times and once more fed into the mangle to squeeze the water out once more. Then it was ready to hang outdoors on the wire washing line. This chore took half the morning. Eventually the clothes and sheets were blowing vigorously in the strong wind. The sheets were flapping and Jack's shirts were dancing about as though he was still in them.

Jack's cousin Cope and his Uncle Ned were coming to tea. They were having lunch with another branch of the family who lived in Otford.

Mathew came running to the door from the cowshed.

"Missus, your washing's blown away," he told Queenie. "It has gone into the woods."

They all went to rescue the clothes which had come off the line in the strong wind.

It was all retrieved at last.

"Thank goodness it hasn't got dirty again," said Queenie. They were all out of breath. Matthew left, laughing.

"It's just another day in the life of a farmer's wife!" Queenie called out.

Then she noticed her daughter. Although the washing had remained clean, Jean, as usual, had not. She had got green lichen on her socks and all sorts of foliage in her hair.

Queenie sent Jean to brush her hair. As Jean only had a limited amount of clothing, due to rationing, Queenie had to try to brush the grime off the clothes with the child still in them. She had wanted her to look neat and tidy for the visitors.

At half past three Cope and his father arrived and Jean waited on the front door step, watching shyly as they approached.

# Hairy Beards.

Jack escorted his Uncle Ned and Cope into the farmhouse. Jean stood behind the front door and looked on as her mother gave them a kiss on the cheek.

"Come on, me dear, give me a big hug," said the little old man who must be Uncle Ned, and he slapped a big wet kiss on Queenie's cheek.

Jean watched in dismay because this man had hair all over his face and it tapered down to a long point where his chin should have been. As he spoke his long, hairy chin wagged. He spotted Jean and made a bee line for her.

"This must be little Jean," he waggled the monstrous chin at her.

As he got nearer Jean panicked. Ned held out his arms for a hug and his chin came up closer and closer. She had never met a man with a beard and she was really scared of it touching her. She ducked underneath him and fled out of the door. Ned ran after her calling out her name and Queenie, Jack and Cope followed. Jean looked back and saw the chin gaining on her. She ran around the corner of the house and it followed. She headed towards the big yew tree in the copse and climbed into the branch that grew under her beech tree. She scrambled along the branch and swung into the safety of her beloved beech. She climbed so high that she disappeared among the top most branches; safe at last.

Although they called her and her father sounded quite cross, she stayed there for at least an hour, swaying about with the strong wind moving the boughs from side to side. It was wonderful. The family left her there and went indoors.

Jean would have remained in the beech tree but she felt her tummy rumbling and remembered the special tea that her mother had laid in the sitting room. Soon the fear of the chin was overcome by the fear of missing the food and she climbed down and slipped unseen into the kitchen where she waited with Tubby until her mother came and found her.

"You are a naughty girl," admonished Queenie, "Why did you run away like that?"

"That man was going to touch me with his horrid hairy chin. I'm frightened of that waggling chin."

"Don't be so silly. He has a beard. Lots of old men have beards. They just don't shave like Daddy does that's all."

"I'm hungry. Have you had tea?"

"Not yet. You'll have to apologize to the uncles first."

Jean clutched Queenie's skirt as they left the safe kitchen and stepped into the sitting room where the dreaded chin was sitting on Queenie's best blue over-stuffed settee.

"Here she is. She was a little nervous at being kissed that's all. Say you're sorry Jean."

"Sorry, Uncle Ned," said Jean in a tiny whisper, still clinging tightly to the safety of the skirt.

Uncle Ned and his son gave her big smiles and laughed. They made no further attempts to kiss the little mite. Tea was eaten but Jack was wearing his stern face.

Uncle Ned gave Jean a half a crown and winked at her.

"There's a lot of Cornish spirit in that child," he said as they left to drive off in the car that had brought them. "Be proud of your Cornish heritage, girlie. You are the last Pearce in the line you know."

Jean did not know what he meant and determined to ask her mother.

When she asked what the expression, "last in the line of Pearce's," meant, her father explained.

"Our family tree dates back to the year 1722, when my great, great, great, grandfather first traced the records of our family. Ever since then there has been a son to carry on the family name. Me, my dad and so on back all those years. As my only child you are the last of the line."

"Why aren't there any more Pearces?"

"We have had a shortage of boys being born. My cousin from Cornwall only had a daughter and she married so her children are named Pyne, not Pearce. We'll have to hope Uncle Frank has a son one day."

"I can carry on the family name."

"No, when you marry you'll have a new name and the Pearce name will die out."

"I won't get married then."

"Then you won't have a son either."

"Can't my cousin Frank do it?"

"No; he is a Bellingham. A name goes on through the male side of a family."

Jean thought about that for a while. "Then you'll have to have another little boy."

Jack and Queenie looked at each other and chuckled.

"It's time for bed," said Queenie.

That night, Jean had a nightmare about her father suddenly growing a beard. She woke up and went down to their room and clambered inside the shelter.

"I'm scared," she moaned, "and I'm cold."

Queenie got up and made the child a warm drink of milk and tucked her up again with the warm china hot water bottle by her feet.

"Go to sleep now."

"Night, night, mummy dear, see you tomorrow." mumbled Jean.

The next day at school, the teachers had dreamed up another ordeal. Vaccinations! The children had to line up, class by class at the bottom of the staircase.

Terry Pitman delighted in telling the younger ones.

"You have to go up by yourself and have a huge needle jabbed in your arm."

"Don't be so nasty," said John Peerless, one of the bigger boys. Some of the boys were really nice; like Peter Leadbeater and Terry Martin. Others like Terry Pitman and Spud Murphy were always teasing the younger ones.

Many of the children were crying when they came back down. Some were crying before they went up! Jean was determined to be brave and she was. It was only a little prick with a needle after all. She had been in more pain when she fell over on the gravel. Later on though it began to throb and swell up and look red. The girls in her class began comparing their wounds.

When Jean got home she began to bombard her mother with questions about the Pearce family.

"Ask your father."

Jean waited until Jack had had his tea and then sat on the arm of his old armchair, which she knew had belonged to Grandfather Pearce. He had died in the January of the year that Jean had been born. She was supposed to have been the boy to carry on the family name of course.

"Tell me about Granddad," she began.

"He was born in Cornwall and came to London to make enough money to buy back the farm that his younger brother had gambled away. The shame of it had killed Granddad's father. My father got a job at the Woolwich Arsenal and helped make weapons shortly before outbreak of Boer War. He met and married my mother who came from London. By the way, did I tell you that Grandma was born within the sound of Bow Bells?"

"What does that mean?" Jean interrupted.

"If you are born where people can hear the bells of St. Mary le Bow church in Cheapside, it means you are a True Cockneys."

"So Grandma's a cockney like Auntie Elsie?"

"You could say that. She is very proud to be a cockney even though she doesn't sound like one."

"Go on," said the eager child.

"Where was I? Ah yes, so Granddad worked hard for twenty five years. When I left school I worked in the drawing-office at the Arsenal too, by the way. I earned a solid gold sovereign for my first week's wage, and I've still got it!" Jack said proudly." Then I met your Mother and we courted for a while and then my Dad found that the Titsey Estate was selling off pieces of land for farming. We came down here to look over the property and decided to buy this parcel of land. We came down here to live. We had to build the farmhouse first and then I built this house so your Mum could marry me and live here too."

"I always thought our house was old."

"No, it was built in 1928."

"Why didn't you all go back to Cornwall?"

"Connerdown property was divided up, and none of it was for sale."

"I'm glad, I love it here. Show me the sovereign?"

"It's in the tin box in my bedroom. Pop along and fetch it. I'm too tired."

Jean flew to look in the tin box which contained items that Jack deemed special. There it was; a beautiful coin. She noticed that a dragon was stamped one side and a man's head was embossed on the other side.

She carried it to her dad, who held it in his calloused hand and remembered how proud he had been on that first pay day. It gleamed in the firelight.

"It's so shiny," said Jean.

"It is made from solid gold, the most valuable metal in the world, they say. The Romans, Greeks and Egyptians all treasured gold above all other metals."

"Is Mummy's ring made of gold too?"

"Yep, your Mother cost me a fortune," chuckled Jack.

"Tell me more about the family."

"Granddad worked so hard to save for a farm that he became ill. He had several strokes and then he died in 1936 and I had to take over the work on the farm. I'm very proud of my Dad's achievement though. It wasn't easy even in those days to save up enough to buy a farm and stock it from scratch; especially with a wife, three children and a mortgage."

Jack was quiet for a while, deep in thought. His Dad had been a stern man and Jack found it hard to show his feelings. They had still managed to hold on to the farm even though it been a hard struggle, especially during and after Jack's own illness.

"Would you like to hear my Dad speaking?"

"But he's dead!"

"The BBC made a gramophone record called, "Daybreak on a Surrey Farm." It was our farm and you can hear my Dad's voice on it."

They wound up Queenie's gramophone and played the record. First they heard the dawn chorus and then various farm noises including chicken and cows. Then Jean heard a man's voice; her Granddad speaking to the pigs. "C'mon C'mon. Get over," his voice came back from the dead. It was scary.

Jean was enraptured and listened to it over and over again.

"I'm going to write a composition about it all. Miss Towler told us to write a story."

"Good idea," said Jack.

The rest of the evening was spent with Jean asking questions about the various ancestors. One of these in particular, intrigued Jean; his name was Edwin Pearce. He had been stupid enough to get into debt and to pay his creditors his father had to mortgage Connerdown Farm, their family estate in Cornwall. The worry and shame of it all caused my Granddad to have a stroke. He died soon afterwards. The estate had to be sold to pay the mortgage and death duties and my father set off to make a new life in London. He hoped to make a fortune but that didn't happen."

"Poor Granddad," said Jean, who was taking it all to heart.

"As I said, he got a job at The Arsenal, married your Granny Pearce after a whirlwind romance, and they settled down to live in Eltham. He bought the house in Earlshall Road where I was born. Uncle Frank and the Auntie Doris came along later and we all lived there until Granddad had saved enough to buy another farm; you know the rest."

"What happened to Uncle Edwin?"

"I heard that he went to Australia and became a vicar."

"But he was a bad man!"

Jack laughed. "My Uncle Edwin was a fool. Luckily I've never met him; good riddance I say."

"Who was Uncle Edwin?"

"He was my father's younger brother."

"How did he get into debt?"

"He was silly and got in with a rich crowd. He tried to live like the gentry and played cards for money he didn't have."

"I won't ever play cards for money," Jean was thinking of Happy Families and Snap.

At school the next day, Jean wrote about Uncle Edwin's exploits in composition time.

"This is interesting, Jean," said her teacher.

"We were very rich once, Miss," said the child proudly.

"Really," replied Miss Towler.

At playtime the other children called her a show-off. She didn't care.

For several years Jean felt as though she came from a posh family. She was basking in the former glory of her land-owner ancestors, who it turned out, were quite ordinary farming stock really.

# Going to London to Visit the Queen.

Queenie had been invited up to London to visit her best friend Ruth, during the Whitsun half term break. Jean was wearing the nicest clothes she had; hand me downs from Ruth's daughter Christine. They set off for London on the train. It was the first time Jean had travelled so far. It seemed to take for ever. The train puffed and chugged through lots of tunnels and past loads of stations and each station was bigger than the last. When they reached Croydon they got off and changed trains. Jean saw three other trains all at once and they had lots of carriages.

"Why don't they bump into each other?"

"The signalman makes sure they are all on different tracks, darling. Don't worry."

They boarded the train to London which had little tables in between the seats. Looking out of the window, Jean saw so many houses she could hardly believe her eyes. They were all stuck together in long rows.

"Where are the fields and woods?"

There are some here and there. We're passing through the outskirts of London."

"Why are there so many houses?"

"Because people have all come here to live and the houses had to be built for them."

"Who would want to live here?" Jean scoffed, "I wouldn't."

"Shush dear," said Queenie, as people were staring at them. "Lots of people would hate to live in the country, and these people have jobs up here in town."

As they finally drew in to the huge station Jean held tightly on to her mother's hand. She had never seen so many people and they were rushing about in the smoke and the noise of Victoria Station. Queenie felt quite at home because until Jean had been born she had come up to Victoria every weekday to work.

Queenie took Jean to visit her old employer's establishment. The establishment was still there, the bombs had not hurt the block of offices. Jean was introduced to Miss Marks who had been a close friend of Queenie's.

"What a sweet child you have here, Edith," said the funny old lady, pressing a florin into Jean's little hand which to Queenie's dismay was extremely dirty even for Jean.

They did not stay for long at the solicitor's office as Miss Marks was working.

They went down to the subway station. First they stood on a moving staircase and then they went down a windy tunnel deep, deep, down under the depths of the city. There was a constant droning noise and rushes of warm air blew Jean's hair about.

"Why is it so windy down here?"

"I think it has something to do with the trains rushing through the tunnels," said Queenie.

The trains here were different and extremely loud. They came along so fast and travelled along the tracks with a lot of wobbling and swaying about. Some people had to stand as the carriage was so full. Jean did not like being down there.

"How far is it?" she asked "I want to get off." Jean was sitting on Queenie's lap and the standing passengers were so close to her face, she felt trapped.

"It won't be long, darling."

"Who dug all these tunnels? I can hardly breathe."

"I have no idea. Don't make a fuss. Poor Peter and Wendy have to spend hours down here when there's an air raid,"

"Ah, so THIS is the underground!" suddenly Jean knew what Peter had been talking about. It was certainly not as she had envisaged it.

Once they left the underground it was only a short walk to the elite neighborhood where Roly Mathez and his family had lived together before the war. Roly was now absent in Switzerland.

Finally they arrived at Ruth's town house in Hendon. It was very posh and had gleaming parquet wood floors. The Mathez family was quite well to do, as Queenie put it. Roly was a stockbroker.

"It's so lovely to see you, "Ruth gave her friend a big hug. Ruth had grown up with Queenie and there were no airs and graces about her.

"Hello Jean. Oh Queenie isn't she like Jack? There is a little bit of you there too, I can see she has your cheekbones," she added.

Jean said hardly a word. She was terribly shy with strangers. Christine was a year older. She let Jean play with her toys, although they were not the sort of things Jean usually played with. The food was nice. Ruth told them that she got some of it on the black market.

After a really nice tea, eaten off fine bone china, and with napkins that Jean had mistaken for handkerchiefs, the two old friends chatted about all sorts of things that Jean had never heard of.

Ruth and Queenie had been friends since school. When Queenie's mother had died, her father had remarried. This had hurt Queenie deeply and she left home to stay with Ruth and her family until she married Jack and moved to Oxted. Ruth went to live in Hendon after her marriage to the man from Switzerland that Jean would never meet.

Queenie never forgave her father, for marrying a young girl in her twenties. Queenie was nineteen years old herself at the time. Her mother had recently died; so recently that she considered it shocking behavior and told him so. Her father had told her bluntly that the lovely lady, who had brought Queenie up, was not her real mother. He said that his wife had been barren.

These discoveries had completely overwhelmed Queenie. It was all too much for her to cope with and so she left home never to return. Jean was never to meet her grandfather. Queenie applied to Somerset House for her birth certificate and found that all her father had told her was true. Her birth mother had been a certain Caroline Parrant who came from Farnham in Surrey. Queenie went there once but there was no trace of this individual. Queenie had never attempted to trace her real mother again.

Jean followed Christine around the smart town house looking at all the nice things Christine possessed; but Jean was not impressed by any of it.

"Don't you have a cat?"

"No we don't have pets because we travel a lot and you can't bring animals in and out of England. They have to go into quarantine."

Jean did not know where quarantine was and didn't really care. She did however feel sorry for Christine for being deprived of pets.

"Where have you travelled?"

"We used to spend half of the year with my father's family in Geneva."

"Where is Geneva?"

"It's in Switzerland of course. Daddy is Swiss and at the moment he is stuck out there and the war is stopping us from joining him."

"Is Hitler in Swissland too?"

"No, as a matter of fact Switzerland is neutral."

"What does that mean?"

"They don't take part in wars. It is a very tiny country and it is situated in between France, Italy and Germany so it never takes sides."

Christine sounded so grown up and Jean didn't understand half of what the older girl said, but she'd die rather than say so. However she did admire Christine who seemed to know so much.

It was soon bedtime and Jean slept with her mother in a small double bed. The flat was nowhere near as big as their farmhouse thought Jean proudly.

Plans had been made for the next day. Jean was to be taken to see some of the sights of London. In the afternoon, they were going to Hyde Park for a swim in the Serpentine. Jean was very excited but she soon fell asleep. In the morning when she woke, she wondered where she was; the sounds from outside were so different from the friendly country bird-song and the gentle lowing of the cows in the field. Then she remembered and couldn't wait to get outside to see London.

Ruth took a taxi into London and thus began Jean's adventure in the capital.

Queenie proudly showed Jean all the sights; beginning with Buckingham Palace. Jean stared in wonderment at the King's home. It was huge. Jean had never seen such a large building; it was absolutely magnificent. The royal flag was flying which meant that the King and Queen were still there, Ruth told them.

"The two Princesses have gone to Windsor Castle, where they will be safe," Ruth added.

She knew a lady whose daughter worked at the palace. Winston Churchill had suggested that the Princesses should go abroad when war broke out but their mother absolutely refused to allow it.

Queen Elizabeth had replied, "The children won't leave without me. I won't leave without the King and the King will never leave."

When Queenie heard this little tale, she felt the tears well up; she was very touched by the Queen's brave words. The King was the figurehead of the British people and he and his family were enduring the same hardships as the rest of his subjects. Buckingham Palace had been bombed twice in 1940 and the chapel had been destroyed. King George had been off to see the troops and boost their morale.

He had fought against the Germans in the First War, at the battle of Jutland, but he was not allowed to go to the front during this war in case he was killed or captured.

Jean learned a lot during her trip to London so far and was all ears to hear more. After leaving the Palace they went to see the Tower of London. This fortress had been built in 1078 and new parts had been added in later years. They were not able to go inside the actual building. Jean was fascinated to see the place where Ann Boleyn had had her head chopped off by Henry the Eighth. They trooped off to Hyde Park next, and had a picnic. There were a lot of people there and several were swimming in the lake which was called the Serpentine. Queenie dressed Jean in a salmon pink bathing costume which she had knitted before their trip using wool from an old cardigan of her own. Lots of Londoners swam in Hyde Park; swimming pools were unheard of. Queenie and Ruth had both swum there on many occasions.

Jean didn't need a costume for swimming in their river. However Queenie did not want Ruth to think that Jean didn't have a swim-suit and so she knitted one especially for the trip. Queenie's costume was ages old but decent enough. They donned their swimming costumes and then they all went down to the water's edge. Although it was a hot day for Whitsun, the water was not as warm as it had looked, and they waded in gradually. Queenie was a good swimmer and she swam in a way Jean had not seen before; she called it the side-stroke.

"I didn't know you could swim mummy!"

"I learned when I was a little girl. I used to swim right here when I was young."

"Why don't you come up the triangle with us?"

Queenie laughed, she wouldn't say why not but Jean assumed it was because of the presence of the cows in the meadow beside the river.

They splashed about in the lake until finally Jean plucked up enough courage to get her shoulders under water and she swum a few strokes proudly before putting one foot on the bottom again. She could only manage a few tentative strokes but Queenie praised her.

Everything was fine at first but then Jean's swim-suit began to feel heavy. Queenie and Ruth soon left the water and wrapped themselves in Ruth's luxurious Harrods's towels.

"Don't go out of your depth, Jean," called Queenie.

"I want to come in now," said Jean. Her suit was getting heavier all the time; the wool had absorbed lots of water. She walked with difficulty towards the shore of the lake, and the lovely pink suit began to stretch. The costume stretched appallingly with the weight of the water that it had soaked up. Although the straps were still over Jean's shoulders the bottom of the suit hung low around her ankles. Queenie was frozen, unable to believe the sight. Some other children began to point and laugh at the naked, woebegone child. Jean burst into tears of embarrassment and her mother rushed down the bank to wrap her up in a large, fluffy towel. They left the offending garment in a waste bin in the park; neither one of them ever wanted to see it again. Ruth gave Queenie one of Christine's to make up for it.

In the evening Ruth took the visitors to the theatre as a treat and to make up for the disaster at the Serpentine. They saw a children's play called, "Where the Rainbow Ends." It was a lovely little story about a group of children on a quest. Jean did not know what they were searching for but was intrigued by the fact that they had to carry all their "sins" on their shoulders until they were forgiven by God. Well that's what Jean thought it meant. She determined to be good in future in case she had to carry a burden like that on her back. These burdens were covered in feathers and seemed very heavy. The people were bowed down by the weight of them and some burdens were absolutely huge. They were held in place by nasty claws that stuck into the flesh of the children in the front of their shoulders.

"I promise to be good and I won't tell any more fibs, Mummy." whispered Jean on the way home.

"I'm sure you will be good darling; we'll see," said Queenie, wondering how long that promise would last.

They travelled home the next morning. Jean could not wait to tell Frank and Joyce all about London.

They arrived back at tea time and Jean wasted no time before rushing to see Frank.

"I saw the palace where the King and Queen live."

"Did you see King George?"

"Yes," she said without batting an eyelid. "He was in the palace."

"I bet he wasn't," Frank grunted. He was used to Jean's tall stories. "I'm going to ask your mum."

"She didn't see him. He was inside and he looked out of the window at me."

"How do know it was him?" asked Joyce.

"He had a crown on his head of course!"

Frank didn't know whether to believe her or not but at least she had been to London so it might be true.

"I saw the Tower of London and Ann Boleyn's head, well not exactly her head but where it fell off, there was a lot of blood."

"Gosh, how much blood was there? I'd like to see that. What else did you do?"

"We went swimming in the park, and we went to see a play." she stopped, suddenly remembering the burdens.

"Anyway, I'm almost certain it was the King I saw." she added, thinking that now she hadn't told a real fib. Then she shrugged it off and they all went out to check the rabbits. There were now eight rabbits in the pen because Whiskers and Thumper had got married.

Uncle Laurie said that they must let them go when the babies were big enough.

Tubby sulked at bedtime. He had been worried when Jean had not been in her bed for two days. He sneaked in under the covers and she put her arm around him; all was well.

Jean lay there hoping that her mother wouldn't tell anyone about her knitted swimsuit. Then she was fast asleep. The little white lies and the possibility of receiving a burden were banished from her mind.

# Bicycles, Bricks and Peace-Work!

The Whitsun holidays were over all too soon and the children returned to school. It wasn't too bad though because the evenings were drawing out and Jean could play outdoors for longer. She often went over the road to the brickyard and watched the old men making bricks. It was fascinating to see the deft way they transformed the wet yellow clay into red bricks. It was quite hard work and they were very skilful. The clay itself was dug out manually from the clay pit that lay opposite their farmhouse. It was taken by barrow-load to a great big iron mixer; a large round, low bowl about ten feet in diameter. The clay was tipped in and the tub would revolve slowly. It was powered by a huge motor standing inside a shed. A great, thick belt drove the machinery which made the bowl revolve. There were large metal blades separating the bowl into two halves. The clay was mixed with water and it became very soft and squishy. The blades allowed the clay to run between them and when it was soft enough, the men would collect barrow loads of it. The whole contraption was very noisy once it was in operation. It made a strange clanking noise as it revolved. Jean could hear the sound through her bedroom window.

The men carried the soft clay to benches in wheelbarrows. Then, taking small amounts at a time from a pile of wet clay on their bench, they slapped it into a wooden mould; the shape and size of a brick. They used a wire implement to slice the top off and then picked up the wooden mould containing the brick-shaped clay and empty this newly-made brick on to a long barrow on the other side of the bench. When the barrow was full of soft, yellow bricks, the men rushed off with this barrow transferring the bricks to the drying shelves. These shelves had wooden roof-shaped covers on them and ran the whole length of the "brick-field." Then the men ran back to start a new batch. They worked at top speed all the day long.

"Why do you run all the time?" asked the inquisitive girl.

"We're on piece work," the brick-maker answered.

Jean told her mother that the war must be ending because the men were making bricks for peace.

Queenie smiled. "I expect they get paid by the amount of bricks they make darling."

"No! It's for peace I know that's what he said."

"I know they need to make a lot of bricks to rebuild the houses in London that have been bombed."

Once the bricks were dry, they were transported to the huge red brick stack at the other end of the brickfield. These stacks were much taller than houses and were very hot. They had fires inside them and the bricks were cooked until they were a lovely orangey-red colour. There was always a really horrid smell around the stacks and it made Jean cough and choke whenever she passed it. She would take deep breaths and run past the two immense kilns at top speed so as not to breathe in the fumes. Once upon a time a tramp had slept beside one warm stack and he had "woken up dead," as Frank had put it.

From her bedroom early in the morning, Jean would hear the friendly noises coming from the brickyard. The clackety-clack of the mixer, the rhythmic sounds of the men making the bricks, and she thought of the peace that was on the way.

"What will it be like when there's peace?"

"It will be wonderful. We won't have to pull the curtains at night. We will have chocolates, bananas, coffee, all sorts of gorgeous food, and we'll have a car again. We will be able to go to the seaside. Just you wait and see!" Queenie looked wistfully out across the valley, lost in thought.

"Will it be soon?"

"What dear? Oh I hope so."

Laurie had taken a new job at Gatwick Airport where he was a toolmaker. He was given a petrol allowance for his motor bike and Frank, Joyce and Jean were allowed to sit on it. It was called a Beezer. Sometimes Laurie would take them for rides on the pillion. He wore a tight fitting, leather hat that fastened under his chin. He had brown leather goggles too. Jean thought that he looked just like the German pilot she had seen looking down from his plane when her mother had waved a tablecloth at him.

Jean loved that motorbike and vowed to have one of her own one day.

"When I grow up I'm going to have a Beezer," she informed everyone.

"I used to ride a motor-bike," said Jack. "Your Mother used to ride on the back; I think we've got a photo somewhere."

Queenie got out the photo album and they spent time looking at the old photos.

"You both look much younger," said Jean.

"Oh thanks," said Queenie pretending to be sad.

"Take a photo of me now I'm bigger."

"The rolls of film are very scarce and too expensive on the black market, I'm afraid."

Jean understood; Hitler had all the film as well as the food that should have come into England on the ships.

Jack had found an old push bike in one of the sheds and he cleaned it up and mended the chain.

"You can go to the shops on this, Queenie."

"What about me?"

"You couldn't reach the pedals."

"I bet I could," she argued.

"No, Jean, you can't ride the bike; it's for your mother and that's final."

The bike was all black and Jack eventually made a flat metal seat for Jean to sit on when they went down to the village. Jack gave Queenie the old bike because she'd had a nasty fall on the road by the bridge. She had been playing a game of trains with Jean the previous week, when she had slipped and fallen on to her knees in the gravel. Her poor knees were torn and bleeding. Jean thought they looked like raw mince. Jean had cried because seeing her mother in pain, had made her own tummy hurt.

Since they were near to Ann's house, Jean insisted that her mum went there to wait for her Dad to come and collect her. Mrs Lever had not met Queenie before and she made Queenie welcome and cleaned her knees up. That night, Jean slept at Ann's house which was the first of many sleep-overs. Ann went to Limpsfield School so they were only able to play during weekends or in the holidays.

The new bicycle was wonderful as it made trips to the shops much easier for Queenie. There was a wicker basket on the front of the bike for the groceries. This new bicycle was a challenge to Jean and she was determined to learn to ride it. Whenever her mother was busy and not watching, Jean would wheel the bike into the garden and, with her right foot on the left pedal, she would scoot along whilst holding tight to the handle bars. Frank could already ride and Jean was all the more determined to learn. One evening, she made a real effort and placed her left foot on the left pedal and then swung her other leg across. Suddenly she was actually doing it; riding the bike! Down the path she wheeled along feeling so good, so clever that she whooped out with glee.

Jack and Queenie, sitting indoors, suddenly saw Jean's head flash past the window.

She was balanced precariously on the pedals; gripping the handlebars as she careered onwards   down the slope towards the bottom of the garden and then on into the orchard and on towards the bushes at the other end.

That was when she realized that she couldn't stop the bike. It hit a bump and jumped up in the air. Jean fell in a heap on the ground as the bike disappeared in the bushes.

Jack and Queenie arrived breathlessly as Jean scrambled up proudly.

"Did you see me? I can ride!" she exclaimed.

Jack was so glad to see that she was unharmed that he did not grumble.

He went to retrieve the bike. Apart from the chain having come off, it was undamaged.

"You could have broken your neck," said Queenie. "You mustn't ride it until you can reach the saddle, and that's that! Go indoors; now!"

Jean decided not to argue, she had never seen her mother so upset. Jack followed along behind them, chuckling to himself. That girl was full of mischief but in a funny way he was quite proud of her. She had guts.

Jean cleaned herself up and Queenie gave her a big hug.

"I was cross because you frightened me so."

"Don't be frightened, I always bounce, Mummy. I wanted to ride because Frank can."

"I know, but Frank is older than you and much taller, and he's a boy."

"I know. It's not fair. I always wanted to be a boy too. I want to play boy's games. Girls are so stupid!"

"One day, mark my words you'll be glad that you are a girl."

"I won't, will I Daddy?" the child replied looking at her father with such a strange expression on her face.

"Your mother is right. Anyway, I am really pleased that you are my special little girl. I'm really lucky to have two such lovely girls to look after me."

Jean flung herself at her father quite overcome by his words.

"I always thought that you wanted a boy, Daddy."

"If I had to choose between you and a hundred boys, I would choose you, dear." He held her tight for a moment and then set her down on the floor. "Well there's work to be done," he said getting up.

"Can I help?"

"It's getting late, better ask your mother."

"Go on then, off with you I've got to wash up," Queenie turned away with a lump in her throat. She watched the man and child disappearing into the cowshed, followed at a distance by the ever watchful Tubby.

They fed Dobbin and Duke with hay and water. In a pen in a separate shed Belle was quartered alone, waiting for her new calf to be born. Jack looked her over and decided that the new arrival would not come that night. He gave her some fodder and slapped her hard on the haunch.

"Doesn't that hurt her?" asked Jean, wincing.

"No, cows have such thick skin that if you don't slap hard, they won't even know you are touching them. In fact, a slap to Belle is a bit like a stroke to a cat. It tells her that I'm fond of her."

Jean went up and slapped Belle as hard as she could.

"I love you, Belle. Have a lovely baby."

Jack smiled, and Belle turned her large brown and white head towards them and mooed softly.

Then she turned back to her food and moved her back legs on the hard concrete floor, making a clip clopping noise as she shuffled her huge weight about, trying to get comfortable.

"Poor Belle; does it hurt her when she borns?"

"Cows don't feel pain the way people do. They don't feel fear like us either and if she's not frightened so she won't feel pain. To a cow it is just a natural part of life."

"Will we keep this calf?"

"It depends if it's a bullock or a heifer."

"Why?"

"We can't keep a bullock because it grows into a bull, and I don't need another bull."

"Why not?"

"One bull is enough on a farm."

"Why?"

"Enough is enough! Come on, let's close the chicken pens."

"Is that why we only have one rooster as well?" observed Jean as they approached the pens.

"Yup."

"We had two cockerels last year."

"Not for long though. We had the young one at Christmas."

"Did we? Did we eat him?"

"Yes. He was expecting it; he was very proud to be our Christmas Dinner."

"Was he really?"

"Everything has a place in the world. If we had sold him to the butcher when he was little, he wouldn't have had the fun he did have. He was able to run around the yard enjoying himself for a while wasn't he?"

Jean decided a short happy life must be better than no life at all.

They finished the evening chores and went back to the kitchen. Queenie watched them coming up the path. The man was striding along with the little girl skipping happily beside him, now and then pulling the hem of his jacket, as she asked him her endless questions. Queenie was touched by the sight of them. She made hot cocoa, wondering if she could buy any more on the black market. They sat around the kitchen table and chatted until Jean's head started to nod backwards as she tried to stay awake. Tubby had been sitting by the door for ages. He did not like his routine to be altered and it was long past his usual bedtime. He got up and came over to the table and rubbed his head, first on Queenie's leg and then on Jean's. Next he jumped up on to Queenie's lap and rubbed his head on her chin.

Bambi

Children in the farm yard

Haymaking

Plummers Arms

Queenie & Doris

Steam train

Queenie & Tubby

The Pearce Family

Working on the farm

Queenie & Jean

"If Tubby could talk, he'd be saying it's bedtime," said Jack." Come on, up the wooden hill."

Jack picked her up and carried her up to bed.

The two adults linked arms and gazed down at the little girl in her bed with her cat beside her.

"We are lucky," said Queenie.

""She was worth the wait," replied her husband.

They went out and Jean lifted up the covers just a tiny bit and Tubby crept in.

Everyone slept well as no air raid sirens disturbed the peace of the countryside that night.

Jack's birthday, June 5$^{th}$ arrived; he was forty four years old. Queenie had planned a surprise for him. She'd saved up enough money to buy a beautiful rosewood cabinet that she had seen in the antique shop in Westerham. She cycled the four miles to the little village in Kent and paid for the cabinet some time before. The owner of the shop had promised to deliver it that afternoon, adding on an exorbitant price for the petrol. That afternoon she polished Jack's trophies until the silver cups gleamed in the afternoon sunlight. She arranged his numerous medals on a piece of velvet inside the new cabinet in the sitting room; it had pride of place under the bay window.

Jack had been a first rate long distance runner in his younger days. He had represented his county, Kent, on several occasions. He had won numerous silver cups for his endeavours and his medals were valuable too; four were hallmarked gold. Another of his treasures was a pewter tea set which she arranged on the middle shelf. It made a fine display. She went out and closed the door gently.

Jean arrived home quite breathless from running nearly all the way. It was exciting to be having a party for her dad, especially as it was a secret.

"Can I help you? What are you making for tea?"

Queenie was rolling the pastry.

"What is that for?"

"I'm making sausage rolls for tea. You can cut them up ready to put in the oven."

Together they worked in the hot kitchen. Jean helped her mother lay the table in the sitting room, and noticed the rosewood cabinet.

"Where did all that come from?" she sped over and looked at the gleaming trophies inside.

"Your father won all of those medals and cups when he was a runner. That's when I first met him. He was a marvelous sportsman. He played tennis, swam, and he was in his County athletics team."

"I didn't know that." Jean was very proud and lost no time in telling Frank when he turned up for the party later.

"My Dad was the best runner in the world!" she said.

"How do you know?" said Frank, thinking it was another tall story.

"I'll prove it." She took Frank in to the sitting room and pointed at the cabinet.

"See! Look at all the cups and things, and some of them are real GOLD!"

Frank was amazed and was lost for words for once.

"Fancy that," he said.

Grandma Pearce and Doris arrived with Joyce, and soon after, Uncle Frank turned up with his fiancée Gladys. They all waited in the kitchen until Jack came back from the evening milk round. He was very surprised to see the family gathering and wondered what was wrong.

"Has something happened?"

"Happy Birthday," shouted everyone.

Jack was quite taken aback.

"Is it really? I had forgotten. Good gracious."

Jean ran over and he swept her up into his arms.

"Come through into the sitting room, Jack," said his wife.

Everyone went through to the other room and watched as Jack went over to inspect the cabinet.

"Don't go complaining about the cost," said his mother, who knew her son too well.

"Oh no, it's very nice; very nice indeed." He smiled at Queenie, and gave her a peck on the cheek.

She was content and knew that he was pleased.

"Let's eat," she said happily.

Every one sat down at the old polished oak table covered with a snowy white lace cloth. Although the food was not exactly lavish, due to rationing, it was much better than an ordinary tea. There were hard boiled eggs and a salad in a large glass bowl, sausage rolls on a long bone china serving plate, dainty fairy cakes on a tall cake stand, Grandma's home made pickles and jams, some red and yellow jellies and bowls of preserved fruits. With crusty home made bread and tea poured from the best bone china tea pot, as well as the best china set out on the table, it looked wonderful.

Jean's eyes nearly popped out of her head when she saw the beautiful china.

"Where did this come from?" she asked, pointing to the bone china plates.

"This set was a wedding present. I only use it for special occasions."

"It is so pretty, Mummy."

"What's the latest news, Jack?" asked Laurie, who had just arrived.

"Alvar Liddell said on the news that Casino, in Italy has fallen."

"That'll be the end of Italy then."

"They say that the Russians are advancing towards Germany too," Frank senior commented.

"The Americans are coming from the other direction, to meet up with them. They're all advancing into Germany together."

"Well it certainly looks as though the Allies have turned the tide. We are on the attack instead of defence now," Laurie added. He heard more of the war news, working at Gatwick, which was a military establishment.

"Some one in the village said that the Gerry U-Boats had been wiped out."

"I'm not sure about being wiped out but they've left the Atlantic, which means we are not quite so cut off now."

"Troops can get in and out of our ports at last. Supplies will soon be here."

"That's good," said Grandma, "This is the longest war I remember, and I've seen several."

"Which wars do you remember Grandma?" Frank was very interested.

"I've been through the Great War, the Spanish Civil War, the Boer War, and this one."

"Golly, that's four! How often do we have wars?" Frank asked.

"Too often," said Queenie. "We are such a tiny country I don't know why we have to go to war."

"We are always poking our noses in, that's why!" this comment from their Uncle Frank.

"We have to or they will run all over us," said Laurie.

Queenie sensed an argument developing, as always happened when Laurie and the brothers got together.

"Let's change the subject. There is a football match in Master Park on Saturday. Are any of you going?"

The women were determined not to let the men argue on this special occasion.

"That's a good idea. I'd like to see a game." Doris came to the rescue.

"Football, now you're talking, remember when we used to watch the Arsenal play Jack?" Frank said.

"I remember when Sunderland beat them before the war......"began Laurie.

"Sunderland! There's a pathetic lot........."

"Now they're arguing over football; I wish I'd never mentioned it."

Everyone laughed.

"Let's have a glass of my elderberry wine," said Grandma Pearce.

The children just looked from one to the other. They did not know anything about football league games. All the men young enough to play professional football were fighting for England and the league matches were no longer played.

The children all went out to play; no wine for them.

"I know that peace is coming," said Jean.

"How do you know that?"

"They are making peace bricks over in the brickyard."

Frank had no idea what she meant but didn't ask.

"I want to be a runner like you, Daddy, and win lots of medals," Jean declared that evening.

"If you're any good, I'll train you," he answered.

"It's Sports Day soon and I am in the hundred yards. I'll win, I know I will."

"She has such determination for child of seven, it's unbelievable," said Queenie.

"She gets that from my Dad."

"Well she gets her long legs from both of us and she can run like the wind. Remember when she ran away from Ned, none of us could catch her."

"Maybe she will be a sprinter."

"We'll see. It's time to hit the hay, thanks for my party, and the cabinet is wonderful. How much was it?"

Queenie threw a cushion at his head." That's a secret" she laughed, tapping the end of her nose.

They went up to bed, looking in at their budding athlete on the way.

"See that cat, when we leave, he always gets under the covers. He thinks I don't know," chuckled Queenie,

Tubby lay perfectly still, only a slight backward movement of his ears showed that he heard them.

They went out and paused, and then peeped back at Tubby but he had them taped, and didn't make a move.

"He heard you," said Jack.

"I do believe you're right."

Ten minutes later, Tubby heard the creak of the Anderson shelter as Jack climbed up on top of it. Then he smiled his cat smile, stretched casually, and crept under the covers.

The next day dawned just like any other and everyone went about the normal business of the day completely unaware of what was happening across the channel, for today, was D-Day. June 6th 1944.

They heard all about it on the wireless later that day. The Anglo American troops under General Eisenhower, had landed on the Normandy beaches in France, and after overcoming fierce resistance from the German army; they had broken through.

The liberation of Western Europe had begun. Hitler and his once formidable army were on the run!

There were celebrations in the streets all over Great Britain, people were cheering and saying it would soon be over. The children came home from school early and Jean and Frank burst in to the kitchen, where the families were together.

"Didn't I tell you last night; didn't I?" yelled Jean

"Did you dear?" Queenie was a little bewildered.

"Yes, remember; the PEACE bricks! I did tell you, Peace is coming I said and it has started."

"She did, she told me yesterday too," Frank admitted.

"Well then, you are a clever little girl."

Everyone laughed but Jean was adamant.

"Is the war really over?"

"Not yet, dear; but it soon will be."

"When, Mummy," Jean was so excited that her prediction was coming true.

"When Hitler has been captured, and we capture Germany, then it'll be over. It could still take some time."

The adults could not bring themselves to believe it yet. Still so much could go wrong.

That evening, Belle gave birth to her calf. Jack took Queenie and Jean down to see the new arrival. The calf struggled to its feet and wobbled unsteadily towards its mother, who washed it so roughly; it fell over again.

"Is it a girl?"

"Yes."

"Good. What shall we call her?"

"Well today is a special day so she must have a special name. We'll call her Glory."

# Moonlight Adventure

It was during the warm month of June that the children met the new gardener at Foyle Riding; the big old house across the road from the farm. This house, built in the fifteen hundreds, had several entrances. The central gateway was of wrought iron and upon looking through these gates one could glimpse a spectacular view of the gardens beyond. It was one of their normal assignments on the way home from school to climb up into the old oak tree that formed part of the boundary hedge to Foyle Riding House. The trunk was partly hollow and the tree itself was comprised of two separate trunks from the height of five feet. These two trunks formed a hollow cradle from which Frank and Jean would peer out over the grounds of Foyle Riding. It was part of their routine to leap out of this tree uttering blood-curdling war cries. Sometimes they were pretending to be army parachutists leaping from a 'plane over Germany or France in order to spy on the enemy and at other times they might be Red Indians attacking the wagon trains.

"AYE EEEYA," they cried as they plummeted to the grass below.

They often gazed inquisitively over the nicely kept flower beds and wondered what else was concealed out of sight behind the posh house.

"My dad met Miss Harrison once."

"Who is she, a teacher?"

"No, Dad says she plays a big fiddle, or something; to the nightingales."

"What ever for? I've never heard any music coming from there."

"She does it at night, Dad says."

"Let's go over there tonight and see if we can hear her playing; shall we?"

"What time?" said Jean; excited at the prospect of an adventure.

"Midnight," came the whispered reply. "I'll meet you by the top gate of the farm and we'll go and listen."

"All right; see you tonight. Don't forget."

They scampered off home. Jean went to bed early.

"Are you feeling alright?"

"Yes, Mummy, I'm just tired, goodnight."

She lay awake listening for her parents to go to bed. She knew that they usually went upstairs at about ten o'clock. Soon she could hear her father's snores and lay waiting for midnight to approach. This was hard as she didn't have a clock in her room. Time went by and she waited; trying hard to stay awake. Suddenly she heard a sound on the path outside. She lifted the blackout curtain up a scrap and looked out of the window and there was Frank looking up. He saw her and beckoned. Jean slipped out of the door, pulling on a warm jumper over her nighty. She slipped her coat on and carrying her shoes, she crept downstairs and let herself out of the back door.

Everything looked different in the dark. Little scurrying noises made them jump now and then. They made their way out to the road and walked along towards Foyle Riding. There were lots of tiny green lights shining along the side of the road. Jean bent down to touch one. It was a tiny glow worm. Jean crept along keeping close to the edge of the road. When they reached the wrought-iron gate everything was quiet; not a sound from inside, certainly no music.

"Shall we go in?"

Frank hesitated, if they were caught it would be him that got the blame, but, it would be an adventure and since they had got this far, it would be daft not to go on.

"Yes let's do it," he whispered.

He tried the rusty latch of the wrought iron gates and as the metal lever lifted it made a deafening clank. They froze to the spot. No one came to the door of the house and after a couple of minutes he pushed the gate open. He swung the gate inwards, and it squeaked alarmingly. They slipped through the gap and dashed across the gravel fore-court and into the shadows. They waited, huddled together for awhile but there was no sound from the house.

Suddenly an unearthly scream rent the air. Jean jumped almost out of her skin.

Another scream sounded that seemed to be even nearer and Jean squealed with fear. She grabbed Frank's hand.

"What's that?"

"It's a fox, don't worry I'll take care of you." He had been just as scared as her really but would never admit it. He'd heard foxes before though and recognised the call of the female..

They walked along by the hedgerows separating the various sections of the vast garden. They walked through rose gardens filled with heady perfume. They scampered down a crazy paving path in the moonlight and stopped in amazement when they noticed a swimming pool there right in front of them. It wasn't very big and had a springboard stretching out across the water.

"I didn't know they had a swimming pool here did you?

"No. I bet they don't even use it. They must be a hundred years old."

They stood at the edge of the pool.

"How deep is it?"

Frank leaned over to see and put his arm in the water. He couldn't reach the bottom.

"It must be six feet deep at least."

At the other end of the pool was a flight of stone steps leading down into the water. There were a lot of leaves floating about on the surface.

"I dare you to go in?" said Jean.

"I will if you will."

They removed their shoes and holding their clothes above the water, walked cautiously down the steps. The water soon reached their knees.

"I think it's too deep unless we undress and I'm cold already."

"We'll come back with our costumes another time."

They returned; clambering back over the hedge this time avoiding the creaky gate. They shot off along the road towards home. At their gate, a shadow moved and Jean's heart jumped into her mouth. They'd been caught. But no, it was only Tubby. She picked him up and the two children got fits of giggles. They were actually in pain, trying not to laugh. Frank headed off home and Jean crept in the backdoor and up the stairs. What an adventure.

On the way home from school the next day, they climbed up the old oak and looked out over the lawns again. As they jumped down on to the grass beneath, they noticed a man watching them. He had just come out through the creaky gate.

Jean felt suddenly uneasy. Had they been found out? The man came towards them.

"Hallo," he said, barring their way.

The children had to stop and they stood in front of him,; Jean stood looking at her feet as though they were of immense interest to her.

"Hallo sir," replied Frank politely.

"You live at Connerton Farm don't you?"

"I do," piped up Jean.

"I'm the gardener here," the man went on. "I found this gate open this morning,"

"Did you?"

"Yes; funny thing that. I also found some wet foot prints on the crazy paving by the pool."

"Did you? Might have been a fox." said Frank, looking at the ground in front of him as though the area was of a particular interest to him.

Both of the children looked so guilty; the gardener knew that they were the trespassers. There they stood staring hard at the ground and not making eye contact with him; it was obvious. He grinned.

"Would you like to come in and have a look round?"

"Can we?"

"Oh yes, I've always wanted to go in there." said Jean eagerly.

He held open the gate and they followed him into the gardens. The man was very nice and showed them the pool which they saw was a kidney shape with a spring board over hanging the deep end. He showed them the greenhouses which were full of exotic blooms that neither of them had ever seen before. The gardener named some; he called them orchids. Then he took them to see the ornamental ponds with white and pink water lilies floating on the surface and underneath the plants, hiding in the shadows, the shapes of large goldfish could be seen.

"Crikey," said Frank. "Those fish are enormous."

"They are Coy Carp. Miss Harrison had them sent over all the way from Japan a few years ago, I'm told."

"We're at war with Japan now," said Frank.

"It's hardly the fault of the fish," chuckled the gardener.

There was a kitchen garden full of vegetables right up at the back of the estate.

"This is where I do most of my work," said the man. "We grow all our own vegetables."

"So do we, and food for our cows as well," Jean made it clear that they did their bit at Connerton too.

They returned by way of the pool. In a dirty little heap lay a pile of leaves.

"Someone has taken the dead leaves off the water" said Jean innocently.

"Shush," Frank whispered, hoping the gardener hadn't heard her; but he had.

"I thought if my nocturnal visitors came back in the daylight for a swim, they wouldn't fancy swimming amongst dead leaves."

"How did you know it was us?"

"I didn't; until I saw you. Then it was obvious; you looked so guilty," he said with a smile. "Can you both swim?"

"I can." answered Frank, feeling relieved that they weren't in trouble after all.

"I can swim a bit," Jean added.

"Go home and ask your mother if she will let you come over for a swim now, while I can keep an eye on you."

The children ran home to ask their mothers and after Queenie and Doris double checked with the gardener, the party of five went over for a swim. Joyce had a rubber inner tube to keep her afloat. It was such fun. Even Queenie enjoyed the spree and she swum about in the pool quite expertly, surprising them all. Doris did a marvelous breast stroke and shot up and down the pool very quickly. Frank tried to keep up but couldn't. Jean dog paddled in the shallow end until she gained confidence and Joyce floated about on her big black car inner-tube.

Doris stood on the springboard and bounced up and down and then dived in.

THWACK! She hadn't dived in years and did a "Belly flop." Undeterred, she got out and tried again. This time it was perfect and they all cheered.

"Teach me to do that, Mum," cried Frank. He had no idea that his mum could dive so skillfully.

Doris taught him what to do and gradually, after several failures he did a reasonable dive.

They stayed for about an hour and then, after thanking the gardener, they went home for tea. What fun it had been.

"How did you meet the gardener?" Queenie asked.

"He saw us walking home and asked us if we'd like to see the grounds," This was near enough the truth, Jean believed. She still worried about those burdens.

During that summer, swimming at Foyle Riding was a frequent event.

June passed, July followed and the schools broke up for the summer holidays.

There was an air of anticipation during those summer months. Everyone tuned in to the wireless at the crack of dawn and last thing at night. The enemy was retreating back towards the Fatherland, as the Germans referred to Germany, their homeland. Everyday, it seemed that the allied troops were nearing Paris.

Meanwhile life on the farm went on pretty much as usual.

The children spent a lot of time playing in the clay pit. One day after a week of heavy rain, they were investigating the steep cliff and discovered that it had become very, very soft. Frank sunk right down into the wet clay and Jean had to pull him out. One of his wellington boots got left behind in the heavy clay however. With a lot of digging, using sticks and their fingers, they finally managed to get it out. They discovered that under the soft wet part, the ground was solid. They were not likely to sink right in and disappear. The cliff-face had been dug out by decade's worth of brick workers, and was some twenty feet high. It was a favorite game for the two older children to swing on the loose tree roots that hung down from above, and while they were swinging one day, Jean lost her grasp of the wet, muddy root and with a shriek began to hurtle down the muddy sloping bank. Thump!! She landed on her feet and began to sink into the waterlogged clay. It had oozed right up to her knees before she stopped sinking. Although trapped, she was unhurt. She was wedged in to the clay but not quite upright; kind of at a horizontal angle. She was also slightly winded; the breath knocked right out of her.

"Are you alright?" Frank shouted, hanging one-handedly from a tree-root.

She didn't answer. He would have to go down. He turned and laid on to his back and let go. He began to slide down the bank, gathering momentum until he was out of control. He shot past the little girl who was trapped in the deep mud and still sticking out at a strange angle from the cliff face. Whoosh! He carried on sliding to the bottom where he landed in a puddle and sent up a spray of yellow water.

"That looked spiffing!" Jean yelled.

"I thought you were hurt!"

" I'm not hurt; just stuck. Come up and get me out."

Frank clambered back up to rescue Jean. When he got there she burst out laughing.

"You're all yellow."

"What do you mean?" He ran his hand over his face which spread yet more mud on to his already muddy countenance.

"That's made it worse," Jean was in fits of giggles and as she stood there defying gravity.

"I want to do that again. I felt as though I was really flying."

"I really thought you'd broken your leg or something. You didn't even yell out."

"I couldn't seem to speak. It jolted the air out of me a bit. Come on; help me get out. We can slide down again."

Frank pulled and tugged and suddenly Jean popped out of the mud. They climbed back up the cliff, slipping and sliding about as they went up. This time Jean stood on the cliff edge and actually jumped, her arms waving as she tried to "fly." Down she went until her feet once again hit the soft mud which prevented her from tumbling all the way down. The soft oozy clay broke her fall.

"Come on its lovely."

"I'm coming!"

Frank launched himself out into space and, SPLOSH, he landed a few feet from her.

"Isn't it marvelous?"

"It's jolly good!"

"Let's do it again."

They performed this "flying into space" procedure several times, trying to out-jump each other. The original pathway down the cliff became a smooth slide and they went sliding down at tremendous speeds into the water at the bottom.

"Can I have a go?" Joyce had been sitting under a tree watching them.

Frank thought about it for a moment, she looked so clean. Well, he was going to get into trouble anyway, so she might as well go home as yellow as he was.

"Hold my hand then," he cried.

With Joyce in the middle and Frank and Jean each side holding hands, all three of them began to slide down the slippery yellow bank of clay. They would not let Joyce jump off the edge though.

"You're too small. You'd sink in up to your neck."

"I don't really want to jump off," said the nervous Joyce, although it did look rather exciting.

After an hour, the children were really worn out.

"Look at our clothes," said Jean.

"We really are in trouble this time."

"Let's try to wash the mud off."

They went over to the bulrush pond and washed their wellies in the water which was about two feet deep. Jean had the bright idea of swimming in the pond whilst wearing their muddy clothes in hope of removing the mud.

It only partially worked. They went home, three shivering, soaking wet, pale yellow children; their yellow tinted clothing sticking to their bodies.

Queenie heard the children scuffling about outside and wondered why they did not open the door. She put down the potato peeler looked outside.

"Good Lord!" she was almost speechless. On the journey back from the clay pit, their sun-dried faces had turned completely yellow.

Their clothes were dripping water and yellow pools were forming on the doorstep.

"I'm sorry, Mummy. We got a little bit muddy; but we had a really spiffing time. We've invented a new game called flying!"

The words tumbled out and the smile on her little yellow face showed just how much she must have enjoyed herself. Queenie didn't know what to do. One thing for sure, she'd better clean them up before Doris saw Joyce.

"Get out of those clothes. No, undress out there on the step," she said as they began to walk into the house.

Queenie ran upstairs and prepared a bath for the little ragamuffins.

"You girls go up and get in the bath. Frank you can wash in the kitchen sink."

She gathered up the sodden, yellow garments and took them all to the stand pipe in the yard and hosed them down before putting them in the copper.

"I'll have to tell your mother," she told Frank. "You both need fresh clothes."

"I suppose so."

"What were you doing?"

Frank thought quickly. "Jean got stuck in the mud and we all got mucky trying to pull her out." Better not mention the jumping from the cliff. Grown ups never wanted you to enjoy yourself.

"Is that all? It looks as though you've been swimming."

"Well we tried to wash the mud off in the pond."

"It didn't work." Queenie wrinkled her nose.

From then on, when the ground was wet enough to go flying safely, the children took off their top garments and jumped over the cliff in their vests and pants. Queenie and Doris must have wondered why the children's underclothes were such a funny colour, but blamed it on the cheap wartime materials.

"They are all made of shoddy," said Queenie.

"Must be," replied Doris.

# War paint

The day began in the normal way; Jean had been egg-collecting with her Grandma but when she returned home, she couldn't find her mother. Queenie would normally have been in the kitchen, waiting for Jean.

The girl went upstairs to see if her mother was still making the beds and discovered Queenie lying on the floor in her bedroom. Jean couldn't wake her. Jean was terrified. Her first thought was that her mum had been taken ill the way her Dad had been. Had she had a stroke too?

There was blood on the floor beside her and Jean panicked.

She left the house with the tears streaming down her cheeks and huge sobs were making it hard to breathe. She ran down to Auntie Doris's house and by the time she reached it, Jean was hysterical.

"What's happened?" asked Doris.

"My mum, help me, she's on the floor upstairs," the jumbled words poured out amidst the sobs.

Doris quickly ran up to the house to see what had happened.

Jean was crying and trying to explain.

"I can't wake mummy up. Is she dead?"

Doris discovered Queenie sitting on the edge of her bed.

"What happened?" Doris sat beside Queenie and held her hand. "Are you alright?"

"I think I fainted. I'm fine now. Thanks for coming up."

"Sit there while I put the kettle on. Jean was terrified; you'd better put her mind at rest."

Doris made a pot of tea and took it up to Queenie.

"Shall I fetch Doctor Walker?"

"Oh no, I really am much better. It's the usual thing you know; nothing to worry about."

"You ought to see the Doctor; it's not normal to faint. Drink this up and then have a lie down. I'll take care of Jean."

"I want to stay with Mummy." Jean was still frightened that her mother was going to be ill and she wouldn't leave Queenie.

She sat in a chair by the window for a while watching as her mother sipped her tea.

"You are going to be alright aren't you Mum?"

"Yes, my little love, I'll be fine now. By the way, don't call me Mum, I like Mummy better," she reassured Jean with a smile.

Queenie felt better but Jean stayed with her for the rest of the day. Queenie was as right as rain the next day but Jean had been given a real scare.

Whilst helping to clean the chicken coops, a job she hated usually, Jean began collecting feathers. She only wanted the long ones, preferably ones from the cockerel. Here and there, in the orchard and in the hedges she discovered other bird-feathers. Long tail feathers from the jay bird and the magpies were the best as they were really colourful. She wanted to make an Indian Chief's head dress. She remembered the stories that Uncle Alf had told about his ancestors and she'd seen pictures of these Indian Chiefs in the Hiawatha story book.

Queenie strung them together and glued them on a cardboard band and Jean galloped around on her imaginary horse, wearing the feather head-dress. A group of village children encountered Jean one day.

"Look at her!" jeered one of the boys.

"What do you think you are?" shouted another

"I'm a Red Indian," replied Jean.

"No you aren't; you've got a white face."

They all laughed at her. Jean ran home. She disliked those boys from Mill Lane.

She rummaged under the sink in the kitchen looking for something which would remedy the fact that her face was white.

She found what she'd been looking for and clutching a tin of brown shoe polish she ran up to her bedroom. The rusty lid took a bit of prying open.

Jean rubbed her fingers over the slimy surface of the polish until they were brown. Then, looking in the mirror on the dressing table, she applied the polish over her face. Before long she was satisfied; her face was now a beautiful light brown colour. Wearing her feathers, she went back out to play. Now she really looked like a Red Indian!

As the afternoon wore on and teatime approached, she forgot about her face and went home for tea.

"What is wrong with your face?" Queenie stared at the little nut brown face.

"Nothing," Jean retorted.

"It's filthy, go and wash it."

Jean splashed cold water on her face.

It ran down and dripped off the end of her chin. She stood up on the edge of the bath to look in the mirror. Her face hadn't changed and looked rather wonderful, she thought. She tried again with the soap this time. Another look in the mirror showed no change.

"Oh dear," she thought gloomily.

"Jean, what have you done to your face?" asked Queenie upon the child's return.

"Nothing, it's just gone brown. Perhaps I have a bit of Red Indian in me."

"Perhaps fiddle-sticks; perhaps you have been painting your face with something."

"It's only shoe polish. I think it looks nice."

Queenie tried to remove the brown stain in vain; but it seemed to be there for good.

"It will have to wear off. Your face appears to be waterproof."

The shoe-polish began to wear off eventually, so Jean topped it up.

Queenie confiscated the tin.

"You're lucky it hasn't damaged your skin."

"I wanted to look like Uncle Alf."

"What a funny girl you are. Don't do it again."

Jean was rather disappointed that Val hadn't been able to see her squaw-look.

# Harvest Festival.

The long summer holidays were over. The children were back to school and Jean had gone up into a new class. She began to make friends with some of the other girls. They all seemed to know each other well. They lived in the village and could play after school in the playing field together. Jean did not travel the same way home from school as they did and so she was an outsider to them. Even so they mixed during play-times. Several new games were being enjoyed in the girl's playground. Throwing balls against the brick wall was one that Jean loved. They just called it Two-Balls. Carol Martin and Ina Gillingham were very good at this game. Often a ball would go too high and become lodged in the gutter. Jean was able to shin up the drainpipe to retrieve these balls as she was a good climber.

In class Jean was learning new subjects; history and geography being amongst them. She enjoyed these subjects and always listened to her parents when they discussed what was happening on the Continent. She was too young to remember much about life before they went to war with Germany and didn't really understand why it had come about.

The war was turning in favour of the Allies. A handful of German generals had plotted to kill Hitler, but had failed. This news had been heard on the wireless. This gave the British some hope. Maybe the German people were beginning to see Hitler in a new light. Something must be changing for the better in that country if Hitler's own generals were plotting against him. What a shame the SS had discovered the plot! Then, in August, the country of Romania joined the Allies. Jean had never heard of that small country before but decided it must be where the Romany Gipsy people came from. Her friend Sylvia's mother had been Romany. She had lots of polished horse-brasses hanging in her sitting room and had once lived in a caravan. Jean was fascinated by her tales of Romany life; they seemed to be so mysterious.

Fighting in Italy had reached a deadlock and so the Italians not only surrendered but they changed sides as well. Once they got rid of Mussolini, their hated dictator, they joined with the Americans and Germany had no allies left in Europe; unless you included Turkey. Now, the Americans and the Italians were fighting the Germans; the Germans were being pushed back on every front.

"Surely it can't last much longer?" Queenie said.

"I'll bet it will be over by Christmas."

"People said that in 1939!" Queenie retorted. "Thank goodness the fighting in Africa is over. Elsie's John is safe."

"That must have been great news for Elsie? I must write to her," said Queenie

In August the Home Service of the BBC proclaimed that Paris had been liberated.

The beautiful city of Paris had been in German hands since they invaded that capital city in June 1940. Now that Paris had been liberated it meant that the port on the river Seine could be utilized by the allied navy. All of this washed over Jean who carried on living in a happy world of her own.

The French people were free and the British were their new best friends.

"I wonder how long this love affair with the Frenchies is going to last?" Jack wondered.

Britain and France had been at loggerheads over something or other, all through history, Jean was surprised to hear. She was now studying basic history at school. It seemed that Great Britain had had lots of enemies in the past. It was bewildering.

Germany had always been a dangerous foe for that country did just what it liked; invading Poland and poor Holland too as well as poor old France.

Night after night Jean's parents tuned in to the radio to hear the news. Jean listened to all they had to say; trying to make sense of it all.

"Those Germans had no business invading The Netherlands. The Dutch have always been neutral," said Jack.

"I think that Britain should be neutral too," said Queenie.

"We had to commit. We'd signed that treaty which allied us to Poland. We had to wade in when the Hun walked all over them. We'd promised."

"Next time I hope we don't make any promises."

"We will always defend our Allies, and they will defend us."

"Huh. A lot of help anyone was in the beginning of this war when we really needed help."

"Even the Yanks took their time and now you'd think they were winning the war all on their own."

"Well never mind, it's almost over and let's hope there won't be a next time!"

Little Jean took it all in but was getting more bewildered day by day. She really didn't understand what it was all about.

The harvest season was approaching. Everyone was busy on the farm, digging up the crops and storing away the various vegetables for the winter months ahead. Down in the barn was a great big mincing machine. It was for mashing up the mangle-wurzels for the cattle to eat during winter when they were often kept inside; if the weather was too bad. The hay was for the cows as well. Jean loved watching the vegetables going into the large machine and coming out all mushy the other end. The machine made a weird noise as it thundered away doing its job.

Reverend Bray, the vicar from Saint Sylvan's Church, was planning a Harvest Festival for the local churchgoers to celebrate God's bountiful harvest.

Jean was helping to polish the carrots and radishes for the event. Grandma had selected the nicest, biggest, brownest eggs and put them carefully in a wicker basket. Jack collected some rhubarb that grew by the cesspit. Jack's rhubarb was the biggest in the village because of the extra "fertilizer" in that area. The trouble was that neither Jean nor Queenie fancied eating it for the same reason! It would look good in the display at the church never-the-less.

The following Sunday all of the churchgoers from the Staffhurst Wood area went to evensong and admired the wonderful display. There was everything that you could think of. Masses of produce lined the aisles and flowers were beautifully arranged around the altar. There were bowls of tomatoes gleaming red in the light of the tall wax candles. Orange carrots complimented them amidst displays of bright green runner beans. Nests of brown eggs and white eggs glimpsed out from behind the mauve radishes, nestling by the pink rhubarb. There were sheaves of wheat in the background. Vases of chrysanthemums and dahlias, sent by the women's institute gardening club completed the grand display. The wild produce had not been forgotten either, dishes of blackberries and rosehips had their place too. God had provided all these things; so the Reverend. Bray told the children at Sunday school. Rosy red eating apples and green cookers lay side by side with huge onions and all sorts of different varieties of potatoes. Lettuces and cucumber with other salad vegetables were arranged in intricate patterns and bowls of hazel nuts and chestnuts from the hedgerows completed the scene.

The congregation sang hymns jubilantly; finishing with the special harvest hymn.

"All is safely gathered in ere the winter storms begin."

The Pearce family and the Bellingham's made their way home afterwards; proud that they had made their contribution to the Harvest Festival.

"Where does all that food go now, Daddy?"

"I expect it goes to the poor and needy, or the hospital."

"Things don't change much do they?" Queenie said thoughtfully. "I'll bet that the druids did much the same; giving thanks to their various gods for their crops."

"They were just simple folk like us."

"They were Pagans!" said Doris.

"Well they thought that nature provided the crops, and gave their gods gifts to ensure that next season the crops would be good."

"That's as maybe but we know better," argued the devout Doris.

Queenie and Jack smiled at each other and Queenie laughed aloud.

"Tell me, tell me; why are you laughing?" Jean was not going to miss anything.

"Nothing dear, we were just teasing your Auntie."

"Why do we thank God for the harvest, Mummy?"

"We need food to keep us alive."

"Why?"

"Without food in our bodies, well we'd get thinner and thinner and then we'd die."

"So food keeps us alive," Jean was serious. She had never given this a thought.

"Not only that; it helps you little ones grow bigger."

Jean decided to eat all her meals from then on; except maybe not swede.

Back at home they sat out in the orchard watching the sun disappear behind the trees in the brickyard.

"Red sky at night, shepherds delight," said Jack.

"What do you mean?" asked Jean.

"If the clouds look red at sunset and the whole sky is aglow; all pink like it is now, it usually means the next day will be sunny and dry."

"Oh, I see."

Jean slept like a top that night, dreaming that she could fly about in the beautiful red sky, like a bird.

# Renny - the birthday dog.

Frank received a puppy as his birthday present the following April. He shared his birthday with Princess Elizabeth; but she was eight years older than him. The puppy was an Alsation-Labrador cross-breed, and was coloured black and tan. Uncle Laurie said the dog was called a retriever. Renny would go bounding off to fetch sticks when Frank threw them. By September, the pup had grown very big and needed plenty of exercise. Jean and Frank took him to Merle Common for his walks. Since they now had to hang about on the common, they began to explore it a little more than they had time to on school days. There was an interesting tower on the top of the hill. It was called an airway light. It was a tall metal construction with a ladder attached to one side. Once upon a time there had been a bright light shining out from the top. It was a warning for aeroplanes that there was a hill just there. However, because the light would warn the German planes as well, it had been switched off. Now it was derelict. Uncle Laurie had told them that Merle Common was one of the highest points in Surrey.

"It looks like a giant railway signal doesn't it?" Jean was lying underneath the tower, watching ants carrying their eggs down a hole. She had disturbed the busy insect's home when she had picked up an interesting stone.

"Terry Pitman says that he's been up there."

"Bet he hasn't."

"I really think he did because he said that he could see the sea from up there."

Jean was suddenly very interested. She sat bolt upright and, shading her eyes against the bright sun, she looked up to the top of the structure.

"It doesn't look too hard to climb. If Terry Pitman can climb up there, I'll bet we can."

"There's no one about; what do you think?"

Frank went to check the slope leading down to Merle Common village. There was no one around but them. Then he walked out to the road and took a look and called back that no one was in sight.

"There's no one in sight," he called out.

Jean was already inside the wire fence that surrounded the airway light and approaching the rusty ladder.

"Well?" she demanded. "Will you go first or me?"

"I will, but you keep close behind me. We both go up! Come on."

The two of them began to climb the metal ladder. It was at least ten times the height of the railway signal near their home. As they struggled upwards, hand over fist, getting quite breathless, Jean began to feel a little bit nervous. She stopped and looked downwards between her body and the rungs. They were not even half way up but already the ground seemed to be such a long way below. She clung tighter to the metal rungs. Her little hands were brownish-yellow with rust. She looked upwards at Frank's feet above her. He was climbing steadily upwards towards the first metal platform. Taking a deep breath, she gritted her teeth and followed him. As they got higher a breeze sprung up. The wind made a strange whispering sound as it eddied around the youngsters; it turned Jean's skirt into a balloon. Now and then the wind made a definite whining noise as though telling them to go back down. Undeterred, Frank reached the platform and pulled himself up to safety. Jean arrived soon after and he pulled her through the hole and out of danger. They both stood up on the flat platform and warily and looked out across the fields and woods surrounding the airway beacon.

"Golly! Look at the view!"

"Wow! I can see forever! Look there's the farm; isn't it tiny? Look at Oxted; it's like a toy town. I can see right across to the next village. What's that place?" she pointed.

Jean forgot her earlier fears. She turned around to gaze in every direction.

"From up here we can see right across all the ranges of hills stretching towards Brighton." Frank was staring south towards the distant coast.

They peered into the distance, trying to see the sea, but it was too hazy. The far away rows of hills merged with the skyline until it was hard to distinguish land from sky.

"I wonder if we could see any further from up at the top? I'm going up higher."

Frank began to climb the next ladder. "Coming?"

"Alright," Jean's voice wavered a little, but she followed him up towards the next platform. The second ladder was shorter as they were well over half way already. The next platform was really tiny and Jean had to cling on to the rungs while Frank looked about.

"I can't really see much more but everything looks so tiny from up here," he observed. "I'm climbing up to the light. You climb on to this platform and wait for me."

Up he went, avoiding the cables that were swinging loosely in the wind.

"Be careful not to touch those cables!" Jean's words were whipped away in the wind. She thought they might be electricity wires.

The cables were covered in something black but they whipped about a lot in the strong wind. Frank reached the top, looked about and then began to descend again to Jean's relief. Her skirt whipped around her legs in a frenzied manner as she clung on to the rail that stretched around the platform.

"Shall I go up now?" she asked, hoping he would say no.

"No, it's getting dangerous with this wind blowing. You look like you might blow away," he said, noticing her ballooning skirt. "Start going down and wait on the big platform."

She did as she was told. Together on the lower platform they had another look about them. Frank saw Renny dashing about on the ground below. He seemed to be barking at something but they couldn't hear him.

"What's the matter with Renny?"

"I dunno," Frank replied in the slang that all the boys used.

Suddenly Jean saw the man! He was wheeling his pushbike across the common towards the dog.

"Lie down quick; he'll see us."

They lay pressed flat on the platform some eighty feet above the man. He was trying to catch Renny, but the animal ran off into the trees heading towards Merle Common. Eventually the man gave up, picked up his bike and went back to the road and cycled off.

"Phew! That was close. He didn't see us did he?"

"I don't think he did. Who is he?"

"Ernie Thomas. He lives in Staffhurst Wood down near the church somewhere. He knows our parents though. He may tell my dad that he saw Renny running loose."

The two adventurers slowly began the last stage of their decent.

"I'll go first. That way, if you slip I will be able to catch you," Frank told her.

Jean had never thought about slipping, until then.

At last they reached the ground. Down at the bottom of the ladder they gazed back upwards; it seemed impossible that they had climbed up so high.

"Wow, that was simply spiffing," said Frank.

"Yes, weren't we brave?"

"Don't go telling anyone or we'll be in real trouble."

"I won't tell anybody."

They caught up with Renny by following the sounds of his yelps. He was digging out a rabbit burrow and sending clods of earth high into the air with his back feet. His nose was covered in dirt. Frank put his lead back on and they continued down the slope to the hamlet of Merle Common. They stopped for a while to talk to Peter and Joy Edwards who lived there. Joy was swinging on the gate and another child was sitting on the ground.

Apart from the village school, there was nothing but a blacksmith's forge and half a dozen houses surrounding the farmlands.

They stopped by the forge to watch the blacksmith shoeing a horse.

Jean and the Blacksmith had met before. He had saved her finger from exploding once. She had once put a curtain ring on her finger for some reason. During lessons she had chewed it until it was out of shape and was cutting into her finger. The finger had first turned red and later it was blue and then purple. It had begun to throb and became extremely painful. Jean had shown it to Miss Webster who realized the danger had whisked her to the forge. The blacksmith cut the curtain ring off with a gigantic pair of wire cutters. Jean had thought that he might cut off her finger at the same time; but he did not. The nasty swollen finger had returned to normal. The teacher's prompt action and the blacksmith's skill, had probably saved the finger. Jean never did that again.

The two children watched as the man made a new shoe for a huge chestnut horse. He had an iron shoe in the fierce, hot fire when they arrived. When the metal was bright orange in colour, he removed it with a long pair of tongs and put it on the anvil. Then he beat the red hot shoe with a huge hammer and the sound of metal on metal rang out loudly, almost deafeningly in their ears. After beating the shoe he plunged it into a trough of water. Clouds of vapour formed and a hissing noise accompanied the steam. Then he placed the horseshoe back into the fire. This was repeated many times until the shoe was the right shape and size for the horse. The

Smithy had made holes around the edge of the shoe for the nails to go through and into the horse's foot. The blacksmith approached the fine horse and squatted down. He took the beast's hind-leg leg between his own knees and fitted the horseshoe to the hoof. He clipped bits of the hoof away with a knife.

"Ow! Doesn't that hurt?" Jean winced.

The horse took hardly any notice even when the man began knocking the nails into the great hoof. The chestnut gave a snuffling whinny as the smithy's lad took hold of the horse's bridle. The new shoe was hammered home and the horse was led away.

The children said goodbye and collected the tethered Renny and started back towards home.

"Let's go the other way home; over the Diamond fields," said Frank.

Just past the school was a railway bridge which went across the road. They stopped there to yell and shout. The brick walls sent back echoes.

"Hi EEEY Ya!!!!!!" eeey ya.... eey aa. Their voices echoed back hollowly bouncing off the smooth brick walls. There were lots of these places which "made echoes"; one of which was the wall of the cowshed at home.

When they reached home the children parted and Jean went indoors. Queenie noticed that Jean was unusually grubby.

"What on earth have you got on your clothes?" Queenie took a closer look. "It looks like rust. Where have you been?"

"We've been helping the blacksmith."

"Have you indeed? How did you get rust on your skirt?"

"I dunno."

"Don't speak like that, Jean, it's so common. I like you to speak properly! I'll never get that rust off your dress. Take it off; I'll have to soak it."

Jean undressed and went up to her room to find some clean clothes.

"Wash your hands and face," her mother's voice followed her upstairs.

Tubby was sitting on the windowsill, washing his striped orange, rust coloured, face.

"If I had your fur, it wouldn't even notice," she told the cat, as they made their way back to the kitchen.

"Can I go down the cowsheds?"

"Down to the cowsheds," corrected her mother. "I suppose so but do try to keep that dress clean; it's the only one that isn't in the wash."

Jean skipped off to find Susan. The cow was fully grown now and yet she still loved Jean and followed her whenever she could. She would wait by the top fence at four o'clock for Jean's return from school. Just lately, Susan had taken to standing by the fence and mooing in a melancholy way.

"Is she ill, Dad?"

"No, she's calling out for a husband," Jack laughed.

"I didn't know cows got married."

"All creatures need a mate," he grunted.

No one found out about their climb up the beacon. They made the ascent several times during the summer. Each time it got easier and the views were worth the effort. They did realise that it was dangerous and took great care not to touch the cables. Jean was no longer afraid of falling.

As the summer wore on, the children ran out of new places to explore.

All of the children were in the garden with their assorted pets one day. They seemed to be bored. Queenie took a sheet off the line and attached one long edge to the fence wire between the garden and the field, where Susan watched, casually chewing the cud. Using some wooden clothes pegs, bought from a gypsy woman, Queenie made a large tent and the children camped inside with a dish of wild strawberries and some plums. As they played inside the tent, they suddenly noticed that it was getting dark. Since it was only about four o'clock in the afternoon, Frank thought it was a bit odd. He lifted up the edge of the sheet and peered out. It certainly was not dark outside, only inside. Looking up he saw to his horror, swarms of flying ants had settled all over the sheet. Ants swarm at certain times of the year when a new queen is leaving to start a colony. They must have been attracted by the whiteness of the sheet. Queenie heard the children yelling and ran out to investigate.

She was horrified at the sight of the flying insects. She grabbed a corner of the sheet with her finger tips told Frank and Jean to run indoors. Jean was so surprised that as she fled, she swallowed her plum; stone and all. She began to splutter and the stone hurt as it worked its way down her throat.

Meanwhile, Queenie scooped up little Joyce and carried her inside; slamming the door behind her. They watched out of the kitchen window until the ants departed.

Jean was still suffering from the plum-stone effect. She told Frank.

"You know what'll happen now," he said. "That stone will grow in your tummy and next year you'll have a tree inside you."

"I won't! Will I?" She mulled it over and hoped that it wasn't true.

"Daddy," said Jean later that evening, "Guess what? We were attacked by millions of flying ants today."

Queenie elaborated," I've never seen that before. There were so many of them. Are they dangerous? Would they have stung?"

"They aren't like wasps and bees although I believe they belong to the same family, more or less. They'd have got in your hair; that's about all."

Queenie suddenly felt "itchy" all over. She shuddered.

Jack continued, "I read somewhere that there are at least a thousand million ants in the world."

"I thought they lived underground," Jean added, remembering the nest she had disturbed. "I found a nest under a stone by the airway light, and the ants were carrying their eggs down holes."

"When were you up at the beacon?" asked her mother.

"Oh that's torn it," thought Jean, and for once couldn't think up an answer.

"We took Renny for a walk on the common the other day," said Frank, coming to the rescue.

Jean shot a thankful glance which was observed by Jack.

"Don't go playing near that beacon, its dangerous now-a-days."

"We don't play there", replied Jean truthfully. They were very, very serious climbers; it was no game.

"Can we go outside?" asked Frank, things were getting decidedly out of control.

Off they went like the wind, laughing all the way down the orchard path.

"That was close!"

"Yes."

They sat under a tree, eating windfalls. They were careful only to eat windfalls because in late July they had been scrumping the cherries from the orchard and hiding the cherry stones in the glove pocket of an old motor car that belonged to their uncle Frank. Unfortunately, their uncle had discovered the tell tale stones and they had been well and truly told off. They couldn't even deny it because they had been seen inside the car.

"Better give the airway beacon a miss for a while."

Jean nodded in agreement." Grown ups are such a problem," she remarked.

"Aren't they just?"

# Flying Bombs and Cowboys.

The summer holidays were over and it was time for boring old school again.

Frank was studying for his eleven-plus exams. Everyone expected him to get a place in the Grammar School. Jean was almost nine years old. She was glad it wasn't time for her to take exams.

The teachers kept the older children informed, as best they could, about the state of the war. Most people were "glued to their wireless sets listening to the news programme. The children did not have to run and sit on the cloakroom floor during air-raids any more. There were hardly, if any German aeroplanes to be seen in the skies anymore. In fact, it was the American and British Air force planes, flying across the skies on their way to bomb German towns instead. The news programme informed the British people of successful raids almost everyday.

"The boot is on the other foot now," Jean's father remarked one day at breakfast. Jean looked but couldn't see it. Sometimes, she was convinced that her dad must be mad!

In September there was a battle on the River Rhine at Arnhem. The Allies bridged the river in order to cross into Germany and attack the Ruhr Valley towns. This was the area where all the German War Machines were made; the iron, steel and coal towns. The allied planes bombed the Ruhr towns constantly and Hitler's supplies were cut off for long periods; severely damaging his plans. The battle of Arnhem was partly successful but at the loss of over seven thousand soldier's lives. Peace was a long time coming. Germany was fighting for its life!

The army lorries driving to and from the secret ammunition dumps in Staffhurst Wood, drove in and out all the time, carrying loads of bullets, bombs or whatever they had stored in there. The children saw the vehicles but never what was inside them. The heavy trucks were covered with camouflaged tarpaulins.

Jean sat by the edge of the road after school, watching them coming and going. Soldiers armed with rifles always standing on the big running boards guarding the loads. The men would hold to the cab with one hand; their guns slung over their shoulders, always ready with a cheery wave for the little girl. She in turn waved back and copied the signs and numbers down in her red notebook. She also collected car numbers. There were more cars about on the roads these days too. All the cars had badges on and Frank taught her how to recognise the different makes. There were Fords, Austins, Daimlers and a Rolls Royce from the big house, Mollstone Wood, came by every day. Sometimes she spotted a Standard with the little Union Jack on the front.

Just when everyone though nothing worse could befall the British Isles, something even more terrible was in store for the stalwart Londoners.

Hitler and his generals had another dreadful surprise for Great Britain. The new attacks began in 1944. Germany began launching rocket powered missiles towards London. The dreadful Doodlebug appeared in English skies, causing devastation in London and cold fear in everyone's hearts.

These devilish contraptions were flying buzz-bombs, or V1-pilot-less bomb carriers. These awesome weapons were launched from across the channel and propelled towards London. When the flying bombs reached the outskirts of London, the engine would cut out and an eerie silence would follow and the bomb would plummet downwards. Massive explosions occurred on impact, destroying houses, people and everything in its wake.

Towards the end of the war the German boffins developed an even faster rocket-propelled bomb. This was called a V2. These dreadful machines did untold damage to the city of London. Jean often heard them passing overhead. Sometimes they would stop short of London and land in the countryside around the capital. The V2 really frightened Queenie. She had convinced herself that the war was almost over and yet here was yet another, disgustingly clever contraption, invented by the evil self proclaimed Super Race.

"It's going on for ever," she said when they heard about these new weapons.

"Don't get upset. We will win; I just know it," Jack comforted her.

"You've been saying that for five years."

"Soon, Queenie, don't give up hope."

The soldiers tried to shoot down these flying bombs. They set up barrage balloons to bring them down but it was not easy. They were so very fast.

Jean was intrigued by the barrage balloon in the corner of their field.

"It looks just like a flying sheep," she said.

People in Britain had been busy inventing things too. A very fast jet engine had been invented before the war by a Mr. Whittle, and they found a way to install it in bombers and fighters. This made the planes much faster and more able to destroy the German factories. Hitler had one last try. He launched a counter offence against the Allied troops at Ardennes on the Rhine. The allies were held between December 16th 1944 and January 28th 1945. It was called the Battle of the Bulge. After the war it was learned that 77,000 Allied troops and 130,000 German soldiers perished during these few weeks. The German last ditch attempts to stem the Allied attack on Germany failed.

Christmas came and went.

School went on and Jean became very interested in reading. She had read all the books that she had ever been given and joined the library. Her favourite author was still Enid Blyton. The most exciting books were about other children who got up to the same sort of escapades as she and Frank did.

On the odd occasion that Jack and Queenie went out together in the evening, Jean would go to stay with Jack's friend Tom and his wife who lived in Mill Lane. Jean enjoyed these visits and learned to play a game called dominoes. They played shove-ha'penny too. When she told her father he produced an old yellowed box from the disused pantry cupboard where the things like button-jars and the wooden foot were stored. Inside the box were chessmen and Jack taught Jean to play chess.

Jean's school work was beginning to become erratic. She daydreamed all through her arithmetic class. Sums was the one subject which she didn't like or understand. She did exceptionally well in reading and composition, history and geography however.

Miss Towler wrote on her report, Jean has a very vivid imagination which needs to be channeled correctly. For most of the subjects Jean's report stated; could try harder.

The Plaza cinema in Oxted was re-opened. There was a children's matinee on Saturday mornings. Frank and Jean went regularly, traveling each way by train. They were considered to be responsible enough to go alone. The films they saw at the pictures were varied. The programme began with cartoons, followed by a very exciting serial. This serial was called "Riders of the Death Valley." The hero was Buck Jones and he had a friend called Jim. Jean made her friends call her Buck from then on and Val became Jimmy. She ceased to be a Red Indian and became Buck Jones. She still galloped everywhere of course.

"I love Buck Jones," she told her mother one day.

"Do you dear? I used to like him too."

"What do you mean?"

"He's been in films for donkey's years. He is almost as old as I am."

"He isn't. He's only about twenty."

"That film was made long before the war."

"I don't believe you." Jean was quite upset and refused to listen any more.

Not only was the serial wonderful but the theme tune was glorious. One day, Jean heard the Riders of the Death Valley music on the wireless.

"Listen Mummy, that's the music from "Death Valley."

Queenie recognised it as Mendelssohn's "Hebrides Overture". She explained that it was meant to represent the sea rolling in and out of Fingal's Cave."

"No, it's when the cowboys are riding their horses up and down in the Death Valley."

Queenie gave in. She bought the gramophone record. Jean played it over and over until Jack was "Sick of the ruddy thing", as he charmingly put it, "and Mendelssohn's a wretched Hun isn't he?"

"That's not his fault. Anyway Jean loves it and it doesn't hurt to encourage a love of classical music."

Jack said no more about Mendelssohn, and Jean continued galloping everywhere singing "Da-da-dada-da-da," over and over again. "Da-da-dada-da- da!"

Jack shut his ears. He and Laurie had taken to visiting the local pub. They played in the Diamond's Bar Billiards Team. They were both extremely good. Along with their arguments about politics and football, Jean could hear them as they walked home at night up the hill. Their voices were usually raised. They always begged to differ about everything.

"Why do Daddy and Uncle Laurie shout at each other so?"

"Men are like that. That's why there are wars. If women were in charge it would be different."

One day, Jack came rushing in early from his milk deliveries.

"Quick, turn on the wireless."

"Why? What's happened?"

"The Russians are fighting their way to the German border!"

"Oh that's wonderful news."

Queenie and Jack sat by the brown Philco Wireless set and listened as the reports came out over the air. It was true; the Russian army was ready to push on right into Germany.

"Hitler has made the same mistake as Napoleon. Trying to invade Russia was stupid. It is a desolate place and the wily Russians retreat burning their crops behind them. The Germans were starving and the weather finished them off. Serves them right too."

"Yes," said Jean. "It serves them right!"

"I can't help feeling sorry for the ordinary soldier. He has to do as he's told. It's the leaders I hate."

"Don't be silly Queenie," Jack retorted. "They didn't have to follow a man like Hitler, but they did. They only have themselves to blame!"

Jean watched her parents sitting hunched over the big wooden wireless- set determined not to miss a thing.

War makes everyone argue she decided.

"Who are the Russians?" she asked.

"Russia is a huge Country in Europe. In fact it is so big that part of it is in Asia. It is really several little countries all joined together."

"Who joined them together?"

"The Russians enveloped other countries like Georgia and Belarus and Estonia over the years. They all got swallowed up by old Stalin and his cronies."

"Is Stalin the King of Russia?"

"No, they don't have Kings anymore."

"Why?"

"As a matter of fact, when I was young, they did have a King. He was called Nicholas. The Russian people were starving and a revolt took place. The people imprisoned all the Royal Family; even the children and they were then murdered. All shot dead; it was terrible"

"Shot them dead?"

"Yup, every last one of them was killed. Those Russians are nothing short of savages.

"The Russian Royal Family was related to King George what's more; some of his children were about your age".

"I don't like the Russians. They sound just like the Germans."

"You are probably right," said Queenie. "We didn't like them, then, but now we do."

"They are our Allies now."

"How long for, I wonder?"

"Anyway things are looking up," said Jack and he clapped his hands once and went out of the backdoor whistling.

Jean sat on the stairs with Tubby, stroking his soft ginger coat. He was purring contentedly, letting her stroke his tummy. This was bliss, he purred even louder. Jean did not know what to make of all the things she had heard. The more she found out about these other countries, the more worried she became. She jumped up and went back into the kitchen. Tubby fell off the stair as she shot off leaving him behind. He stretched, yawned and followed.

Jean shuffled her feet as she stood beside her mother.

Queenie could tell that something was worrying the child.

"What's the matter, my little love?" she put down her knife and knelt down beside Jean.

"Will someone ever shoot our King and Queen or the Princesses?"

"Of course not; we are civilized. We haven't had a civil war since Oliver Cromwell's times."

"When was that?"

"About three hundred years ago."

"Who was Oliver Cromwell, was he the king then?"

"No. King Charles was a bad king and the peasants, led by Cromwell took away his throne."

"Who were the peasants?"

"People like us. Then we had a Parliament to run the country instead of the King."

"We've got a king now. Did they let him come back?"

"No, they let his son come back, years later."

"What happened to King Charles, Mummy?"

"Actually he was beheaded."

Jean was astounded.

"Are you sure it won't happen again?"

"Germany would have got rid of our Royals if they had invaded us; but they didn't and they won't now, so stop your worrying." Queenie gave Jean a big kiss and a cuddle.

Feeling a little happier, the child went off to find Frank and to see if he had heard the news. It was all very bewildering. It seemed that all countries had wars and killings and it did worry her. She couldn't bear it if anything bad happened to her family.

Jean began asking questions about war and history at school. Miss Towler told them all about the Civil Wars and the American War of Independence, the Spanish Civil War and how wars down through the ages had shaped the future. Miss Towler was surprised to find that her classes were very interested in these things.

The following Sunday Jean had something else to contemplate with regard to all these wars in the past.

The hymn that they sang was "Onward Christian Soldiers."

When she got home she tried to remember the words.

Marching as to war. With the cross of Jesus going on before. Jesus' loyal Army Leads against the Foe.  Forward into battle See his banner go.

She was rather confused because now it seemed that Jesus and God also took part in battles and war.

Just the week after it became more confusing when they learned the Ten Commandments and one of them said, "Thou shalt not kill."

News trickled in during the next few weeks that the Americans had landed on a magical sounding place called Iwo Jima. They had the upper hand against their sworn foe, the Japanese. During World War One, Japan had been on "our side" and China had sided with Germany. In this conflict, they had reversed their roles.

"It's just politics." said Jack.

"Maybe but it makes you wonder if any of them are to be trusted."

"I know and I agree, but it seems that whatever happens, Japan and China are unlikely to be on the same side as each other."

"I don't understand any of it. For instance, why did either of them need to join in? The war was in Europe, not out in the East."

"They like a fight I suppose. I think the oriental people are a bit war-like, always have been. They have had a lot feudal wars going on for centuries."

"It all seems to be coming to a head now. Thank God for our boys and all the Allies."

To Jean and the other children, all of this was just talk. They could hardly remember the days before the war anyway so to talk about it ending, did not have the same impact on them as it did on the adults.

"What will it be like when the war is over?" Jean asked Frank.

"All the soldiers will come home."

"What else?"

"We'll have our old headmaster back, Mr. Weaver. He went off to fight."

"Was he nice?"

"I think so. He was younger than Mr. McCarthy. I think he had ginger hair too."

"Like Pat Dean?"

"Yes, just like hers."

Jean was playing with the big leather baseball that Uncle Alf had given her. It was really too big for her little hands. She was throwing the ball against the wall of the house and catching it as it bounced back to her. She was getting quite good at catching. Just then Jack came round the corner carrying the two pig food buckets. They were steaming hot as he had just collected them from the kitchen where Queenie and his mother had been boiling up all the peelings for the mush. The smell was musty.

"Watch where you throw that ball," he called out to Jean, "Don't break the pantry window."

Jean felt cross, he was always saying things like that as though she was a baby and could not do anything right.

"I won't," she grunted and threw the ball even harder at the wall.

Almost as though it had suddenly developed a mind of it's own the ball swept effortlessly upwards towards the tiny window set up high above, and with the sound of shattering glass, it sailed straight through into the pantry. Frank gazed in amazement, but Jean had turned and headed off into the woods. Before the tinkling sound of the glass splinters reached Jack's ears, she was out of sight. Frank turned and sped off after her.

"What was that?" Queenie asked, but the children had vanished into thin air.

Jean came back at tea time having spent most of the afternoon perched high up in her beech tree, carving her name on the trunk with Frank's Swiss army knife. She noticed out of the corner of her eye that the glass had been replaced with a piece of board. She sidled in through the back door and headed quietly towards the stairs. Tubby was waiting. "Miaow," said he.

"Is that you, Jean?" called her mother.

Queenie came out into the hall but it was empty. She thought she saw the tip of Tubby's tail going round the bend in the staircase.

Jean flopped on her bed with the happy cat.

"Phew. Just made it," she thought.

Later that evening Jack gave her a good talking too about the scarcity of glass.

"You made me do it!" she insisted. "I was alright until you came along."

It was an early night for her.

# Conkers and Newcomers

Autumn approached and the evenings were drawing in. The Red Lane children ganged up together to go looking for conkers.

At weekends and during the half term break, Des and Averil joined them. Des spent more time with the other boys from the neighbourhood but sometimes joined the Gang from Connerton farm. Pauline and Jeannie Russell, from the brickyard were the latest members. They were with Jean when they discovered the source of the little stream that started in a thicket near the house and which joined with other streams to eventually link up with the big river Eden. As Jeannie and Jean were the discoverers, they named this tiny trickle the River Jean.

On one occasion Desmond and Averil Ould joined them and along with Joyce, the children followed the "river Jean" for miles, oblivious of the time it took them. Consequently they all missed tea and arrived home at dusk, exhausted. Des and Averil were in a heap of trouble. They were not allowed to play with the others for days.

Jean had shot up in height and she was now able to climb the biggest beech tree with ease. This tree had a split in its trunk and two huge trunks rose a hundred feet or more skywards. There was a long branch that stretched out for fifteen feet towards the road. Above this branch was another of similar length and it was possible to walk along the lower branch holding on to the top one. The branch was very bouncy and, knowing that the smaller girls could not reach the high branch, Jean made it a "test" for joining her club; the Silvine Club. This club consisted of one full member, herself.

"Okay, Paul, you can join if you swing along holding on to this branch and then drop off to the ground."

"I might break my neck," answered Pauline.

"I've done it lots of times. It's easy; don't be a baby."

"All right, but I want to be a full member."

"Not til you can do all the tests."

"You make up new tests every day that only you can do."

"Well, somebody has to."

"I want to make one up."

"What?"

"I don't know yet."

There was a lot of discussion and several new, easier tests were devised. The Silvine Club had five girl members, Jean, Averil, Jeannie, Pauline and Joyce.

As Frank and Desmond were off with their own friends, the girls were left to do as they pleased.

Winter dawdled along. Christmas was quite exciting. Jean received another new book and some new clothes as she had grown out of nearly everything.

The heavy rain and biting wind heralded in the windy month of March. The people of Great Britain had their radio sets tuned in to the B.B.C. News station permanently, hoping to hear about Allied victories in Europe and in the little known islands off the coast of Japan. The news was often slow in arriving.

Every night Jack would return home and tune in to the Home Service.

"Just leave it to our boys and Winnie," people would say.

Jean knew that Winny was Winston Churchill and that he lived just over the hill at Westerham, when he wasn't staying with the King and Parliament that is.

"I think that Winny was with the King when I saw him in the palace that day." Jean said wistfully, quite believing by now that she really had seen the King

"Don't tell such fibs, Jean," retorted Frank.

They were sitting by the window in Frank's bedroom while he was fiddling with a cat's whisker wireless that Laurie had made for him. This little contraption was making all sorts of whistling sounds as Frank was trying to pick up a particular frequency.

"Can I make something with your Meccano set?"

"No, leave it alone I am in the middle of something".

"I'm bored! I wish we could go out."

"There's nothing to do while this wind is blowing," Frank went on twiddling with his cat's whisker.

"I'm going to play with Joyce." Jean left the room and made her way down the hall to find Joyce. She was in the front room playing with her doll Molly.

"Do you want a game of snakes and ladders?"

Joyce looked up and smiled. It wasn't often that the older children had time for her.

She jumped up to fetch the board game and they sat down to play with Molly propped up beside them.

"I don't like the snakes." Joyce moaned, "Just as I've nearly finished, I end up sliding back down. It's not fair."

"It's only a game," Jean replied sliding her counter up the very longest ladder just a few squares from home. "I'm going to win again. Look I'm almost home."

"Not if you throw a two. There's a snake waiting for you if you throw a two."

"Go on, it's your turn."

Joyce shook the dice hard in the little cup, and threw it out on to the board.

"It's a six!" she exclaimed excitedly. "I throw again."

"You have to move six first," Jean watched as Joyce moved her counter six places and landed on a ladder. "Huh! That's lucky". She watched as the little girl threw again; it was another six.

"Oooh look!" Joyce was positively quivering with excitement as she slid her counter along six more places and shot up another ladder. She was only four places behind Jean's counter. She threw again while Jean held her breath. She couldn't bear to lose at anything. It was a four.

"We're tying now," said Joyce, "Your throw."

Jean took the cup and rattled it with both her hands. She couldn't bear it if she landed on the snake. She threw the dice so hard that it went under the sofa. Reaching underneath she pulled it out and held it up high above Joyce's head.

"Four." she cried out and triumphantly moved her counter to the final square.

"What shall we do now?"

Poor Joyce looked so disappointed that Jean felt sorry for her.

"We'll call it a draw if you can throw a four as well."

Joyce rolled the dice out across the carpet and low and behold it was a four.

"God made it a four for me," said the happy Joyce.

Jean said nothing but suddenly had a vision of a little girl with a burden on her back; its claws clutching over her shoulders. She shuddered.

"Well done. It was a good game," she said, patting Joyce gently on the back.

"Let's play tiddlywinks in the hall."

They always played that game in the hall because it was easier to play on the linoleum. Frank joined them and they played for a while but soon got bored. They were just sitting with their backs against the wall and their legs stretched out across the hall when Laurie came in the front door, dripping wet from his ride home on his motorbike. He stood there and looked at the six legs stretched out between him and the kitchen. He expected them to move and make way for him but they didn't so he stepped over and gave each pair of legs a slap on his way. Joyce burst into tears, Frank took very little notice but did pull his legs up till his knees were under his chin, but Jean was shocked! She leapt up and shouted at her Uncle furiously.

"You horrid, horrid man!" she shrieked at the top of her voice. "I hate you!"

Doris opened the kitchen door at the sound of the wailing and yelling.

"What ever is going on?"

"I'm just teaching these children some manners." Laurie bellowed.

Jean opened the front door and ran out into the driving rain and fled through the gloom towards the safety of her own house.

"I'm never ever coming to your nasty house again," echoed her dismal voice as she disappeared into the darkness.

She arrived back at the farmhouse and burst in through the back door still in floods of tears.

"What's the matter?" Queenie ran over from the cooker and swept the child up in to her arms.

"Uncle Laurie hit me!"

"Why? What were you doing?"

"Nothing, we were all just sitting in the hall and he came in and slapped us all on the legs."

"He smacked you all?"

"Yes, but he smacked my legs twice."

"Oh well I'm sure he will tell me all about it tomorrow."

Queenie put Jean down and went back to the stove and went on preparing dinner. They always ate a proper meal at night, whereas Doris always had the main meal at midday. Queenie always called the evening meal dinner and the daytime one lunch. Auntie Doris called the midday meal dinner and the evening meal tea. It seemed odd to Jean but when she asked her mum, Queenie said that it all depended on who you were and who had brought you up. This of course made absolutely no sense to the child at all.

"Dry your eyes and take off those wet clothes. Where is your raincoat?"

"It's down there! And I'm NEVER going down there again."

"Calm down, dear. I'm sure that your uncle had a reason to smack you. In the meantime you can get dry and help me with the dinner." Queenie had once been told by her old friend Louie's mother, never to fall out over the children, because it would lead to feuds. When families fell out it was very difficult to take sides and everyone would end up being miserable. Jean was not hurt, just offended. The smack had been a shock because she was never smacked at home.

"Have you fed Bambi today?"

"Yes, he had grass and some of my breakfast as well."

"Good girl."

"Where's Tubby?" The cat was conspicuous by his absence.

"He was probably down at Auntie Doris's with you?"

Jean remembered seeing him on Frank's windowsill waiting in the dry place under the gutter.

She flew to the back door and called him. He h ad been waiting under the hydrangea by the door and he sidled in wiping his wet fur lovingly around her legs. He went towards the warm fire which was crackling in the hearth, stopping once to wipe his wet fur around Queenie's legs on his way.

"Oh Tubby, don't do that. Jean, dry the cat, he's disgusting."

Poor Tubby was in a mess. His wet fur was sticking up in spikes. Jean wrapped him in a towel and began to roughly rub him dry. Tubby was annoyed and struggled free. He was perfectly capable of washing himself clean, thank you very much! In fact it was his third favourite occupation after hunting and eating. He retired to the hearth and began. It would take most of the evening but what else had he got to do before bed.

Jean watched him and wondered how it was that cat's tongues did not wear out with all the washing they did.

"Have you laid the table yet?"

"Nearly," she replied although in fact she hadn't even started. Queenie clicked her tongue.

Jean told her father about Uncle Laurie.

"I expect you all deserved it," was his reply.

"I shall never go down there to play again," she told her cat.

March blew itself out and April arrived. Little green shoots burst up from the earth and here and there, primroses raised their pretty faces to greet the pale sunshine. Wooden enemies, as Jean mistakenly called the wood anemones, danced under the trees and the edges of the paths through the woods were lined with dog violets. Bluebell spikes thrust upwards in their millions; pushing through the carpet of last year's dead leaves. It was Jean's favourite season.

On their way home from school the three youngsters left the road to walk home through the woodland. They were always on the lookout for something different. One day they found toadstools on a mossy bank. The heavy winter rain had washed down a bank leaving patches of bare earth overhanging and underneath was this clump of red and white spotted fungus.

"What is it?" Joyce asked.

"I don't know what they are called but don't touch, they are probably poisonous," said Frank sensibly.

"I think that it's a fairy village, and these are their houses." Jean gazed at the elegant shapes of the bright colourful toadstools. Some were tall and pointed and others were broader and flat on top.

Joyce was enraptured and the two girls bent down to peep underneath to see if there were fairies.

"You are stupid! There's no such thing as fairies," Frank scoffed.

"Oh yes there are," retorted Jean. "I've seen pictures in books."

"So have I," said Joyce. "Mummy says fairies die if we say we don't believe in them."

"You're both soppy; soppy girls."

"I'm not a soppy girl!" shouted Jean as Frank walked off without her.

"Come on Joyce." Jean was annoyed with Frank for calling her soppy and pulled Joyce up by her sleeve.

When Jean described the toadstools to her mother, Queenie looked them up in her book. Jean pointed at the red and white spotted ones in the book and Queenie read out a long word and then told her that Frank had been right and they were poisonous.

"He would be right!" snorted Jean.

Queenie looked up and could see from her daughter's expression that Frank must have upset her.

"What's the matter?"

"He told Joyce that there were no such things as fairies, and it upset her, not me."

Queenie smiled and said, "Tell Joyce that there are fairies but nasty little boys will never see them."

"Why are boys so nasty to girls?"

"It's the way they are made. Haven't you heard the poem?"

"What poem?"

"I don't remember it exactly but it goes like this."

"Slugs and snails and puppy dog's tales,
    That's what little boys are made of.
Sugar and spice and all things nice,
    That's what little girls are made of."

Queenie laughed and gave Jean a big hug.

"I love you so much Mummy. Don't ever die will you?"

"The things you say, Jean. I won't die for a very long time."

Jean went outside to play in her own garden. She went over to the new pond that her father and Uncle Alf Hunter had made. They had arranged some large stones around the edge to make a rockery. These small boulders had been thrown out of the earth when the bombs fell. Some were jagged flints but one was smooth and a strange purplish colour.

She began to lift stones up to see if there were any lizards or frogs or even ugly black toads lurking there. She found a yellow and green frog but before she could pick it up, it leapt high in the air and landed plop in the water. Kicking out long legs it disappeared under a water lily leaf. Once they had studied some frogspawn at school and the class had watched the jellyfish mess turn into tadpoles and eventually into frogs.

Queenie came to the door and stood on the step with a broom in her hands. She was looking to see if the chickens were on her lawn. Several of them were pecking about and so she hurled the broomstick in their direction yelling, "Get out of here." She never managed to hit them and they scuttled back into the field. Queenie hated them for leaving their droppings behind where Jean eventually managed to get it on her clothes.

Jean picked up the broom and took it back to where it stood in readiness on the step. She then trudged off to the cowsheds to help with the milking. Susan followed Jean; the animal was now fully grown and expecting a calf.

"I hope it'll be a girl, Susan." Jean whispered to the heifer. Susan was nuzzling Jean's shoulder." Then we'll be able to keep your baby." Jean was already aware that all the boy calves were sent to market, but she didn't understand why. When she had asked about it, her Father had replied that as they already had a bull, they couldn't afford another. Jack left it at that.

Jean believed that the young bulls went to war; it was because of something her mother had said. She puzzled about that as she made her way back through the orchard.

"Maybe the bullocks help pull the guns!" she suddenly cried out to Tubby who had sidled up as soon as Jean had left the smelly cowshed. He detested that dreadful Susan who was trying to take his place in Jean's life.

Having come to a possible conclusion about the destiny of all the young bullocks and bulls, Jean gave a loud WHOOP and did a cartwheel on the pathway. Unfortunately, a chicken or two had passed that way earlier and left a "message" which had now become stuck to her left hand. Jean looked at it with distaste and wiped her hand on the back of her skirt. Then she spat on the palm and rubbed the remainder of the excrement off on a dock leaf. Now her hand was green with slight white and brown smears.

"Bother," she muttered, wiping it off on her chest, where it made a nice colourful smudge on her jumper.

"It's your fault!" she yelled at the chickens which were busily pecking around looking for worms. She ran at them waving her arms about and the frightened birds scattered in all directions, making an awful din. Two of them forgot that their wings were clipped and tried to fly away, only to get tangled up in the sheets that were flapping on the line nearby. The door to the kitchen opened and Queenie looked out.

"What's going on?" she called out, but there was no one to be seen. Just some very disgruntled hens and the ginger tail of a cat disappearing around the side of the chicken coops.

"Jean?" Queenie called, knowing that where there was Tubby, her daughter would be nearby. No answer. The door closed.

Jean was sitting in the undergrowth behind the coops. When the coast was clear she emerged with dead leaves stuck to the back of her skirt, and mud and more chicken droppings on her legs and arms.

"Bother!" she said again. She tried to think of a way to clean herself before her Mother saw her. Jean trudged back to the cowsheds. Tubby jumped effortlessly up on to a gatepost that was over six times his height and sat washing himself until she reappeared.

Jean headed for the dairy. She ran the taps into one of the huge, grey metal sinks where her Granny washed the milk bottles. When the water was deep enough, she slipped off her plimsolls and tucked her skirt into her knicker legs. She clambered into the sink and swished the cold water over her dirty arms and legs.

When she was satisfied that she looked clean, she got out and looked for something to dry herself on. There was nothing to be found.

"Bother!" she muttered again. She liked that word. She decided to dry herself in the wind and ran about the orchard with arms outstretched. Pretending to be a spitfire chasing a German plane, she swooped up and down between the trees and was soon dry. Her skin was now covered in a mixture of smears and streaks.

Jean suddenly spotted something which put everything else out of her mind.

Walking down the drive to the farm were four strangers.

A small lady marched along in front. She had on a purple hat. Behind her were two big girls, dressed in very clean white dresses. Bringing up the rear was a very thin man. He looked like a foreigner; he wore a big dark coloured hat and a dark suit. Jean slipped stealthily behind the remains of last year's haystack and watched silently. Who could they be? What could they possibly want here? A sinister thought crossed her mind; perhaps they were spies! Frank said that the Germans had sent spies over to kill Winston Churchill and he only lived in Westerham, less than three miles away.

Meanwhile, the four spies had climbed the steps and knocked on the back door.

Queenie opened the door and her mouth fell open in surprise.

"Put the kettle on, Queenie", ordered the purple hat. The woman had a funny accent; was it German? How did she know her mother's name if she was a spy? They all disappeared inside the farmhouse and the door closed behind them.

Jean crept out from the shelter of the old haystack. She had acquired a covering of several pieces of mouldering hay by this time, some in her hair but most had somehow attached itself to her woolly jumper. She crept up to the house to see if she could hear anything. She crawled on all fours behind a hydrangea shrub and knelt under the window listening intently. Sounds of cheerful chatting and some laughter came through the open window.

The purple hat was sitting at the table and Jean could hear her plainly. They were not spies but old friends of her Mum and Dad.

"What a pity," thought the little girl who had had visions of fetching Bert Bonnell to capture them and proclaiming her a hero.

"So where is little Jean? I haven't seen her since she was a baby," asked the woman. "I expect she's a little beauty like her Mother now."

"I wish," laughed Queenie.

Jean panicked. She noticed the chicken's mess on her clothes. She crawled from beneath the bush in order to make her escape but a voice cried out.

"I can hear an animal outside the window."

"I heard it too."

"Can we go out to have a look at it Mum? It might be horse."

Queenie's head popped out of the window and caught sight of Jean's agonized face beseeching her not to tell them.

She smiled that "Oh Dear" smile of hers. Why today of all days did Jean have to get three times dirtier than usual?

"No, Poppy, it's not a horse," she said in a resigned voice.

"What is it?

"I think it might have been a little pig," she chuckled. "It's gone now."

Just as Jean was going to make her getaway, Jack came along and plucked her up into his arms.

"Not so fast you little monkey. We've got visitors."

"Daddy, please don't make me go in. I'm a little bit mucky."

It was no good. He carried the struggling child inside, where he deposited her in front of the visitors.

"OH!" said the lady.

"OOOH," said the very clean girls.

The man just laughed as Jean ran across to her mother and hid behind her long skirt.

"How on earth did you get so dirty?" began Queenie as she picked the hay out of Jean's hair.

"Sorry Queenie, she's been helping me with the animals," said Jack coming to the rescue.

"Oh," said everyone in unison.

"That explains it," said the woman, wrinkling her nose.

Jean headed towards the stairs muttering something about the bathroom. At the same moment a ball of ginger fur leapt through the window and landed on the table. The lady jumped up in surprise and screamed. Tubby hissed and arched his back where upon the lady jumped again and spilled her cup of tea over her nice clean dress.

Jean kept running, this time trying not to laugh as she thought she'd probably get the blame for that too.

"Well done, Tubby," she said in the safety of her room.

Jean struggled out of her clothes and was amazed to see the accumulation of foliage that had somehow attached itself to the back of her skirt and jumper. She began to look for something else to wear. Queenie bustled in.

"Look at your untidy room," she said. "I hope Louie doesn't want to come up here."

"Who are they? What would she want to come to my room for?"

"Don't ask so many questions. Just hurry up and get changed."

"You haven't told me who they are."

"Uncle Herbert is a very old friend of your Father's. They went to school together, and they both belonged to Cambridge Harriers Athletic Club.

"When Daddy was a long distance runner?"

"Yes, dear."

"I think that man looks peculiar. Why does he wear that funny hat?"

"Nearly everyone from town wears a hat. It's called at trilby hat. Daddy has one somewhere."

"How old are those girls?"

"Poppy is fifteen and Margaret is thirteen. I can't find you a clean jumper or a skirt."

"Can't I wear my red frock?" Jean thought about the girls in their clean white frocks.

"No, it doesn't fit you any more. I'll have to let it down."

Queenie opened the bottom drawer of the chest of drawers and began to rummage about in it. Suddenly she felt something curling round her fingers and leapt backwards with a gasp.

"There's something alive in there!"

Jean flew across to the mysterious drawer to see. This sounded very interesting.

"Be careful! You don't know what it is."

Queenie was always the nervous "townie", when it came to creepy crawly country things.

Jean flung the clothes out in a heap on to the floor and looked in amazement at the secret that the drawer had been hiding.

"It's my conkers! Look they've got tails!"

Sure enough the conkers had grown tails, long, pale green tails.

"Ooo-er! So they have. How long have those conkers been in there?"

"I can't remember."

"They are beginning to grow. Jean you really are the limit."

"I must show Daddy. Will they really grow into trees? I'll plant them in the copse."

"Don't be silly. There must be at least fifty in there!"

"I collected sixty two, three more than Frank," she said proudly.

"We'll sort it out later. Get dressed. Some of your clothes will be ruined thanks to those conkers."

Finally Jean was fit to meet her new Aunt.

Louie was in the kitchen doing the washing up.

"Sit down, Louie, I'll wash up later."

"It won't take me a moment. I can't stand a mess." Jean stared at her Mother.

"She doesn't mean you," Queenie whispered to the woebegone child.

Louie had a habit, Jean found out when she was older, of tidying up before things even got untidy. She had been known to empty Herbert's ashtray after every single flick of ash from his cigarette!

A few minutes later Louie went to Queenie's hidey-hole cupboard and flung it open.

"Ha!" she cried as everything tumbled out.

"You never change, Queenie."

Jean knew that cupboard well. Whenever the kitchen was untidy and people were coming up the path, Jean and her Mum would throw things inside and quickly shut the door, and then laugh about it. Queenie called it "instant tidying up." Brooms and mops and the ironing-board lived in there normally. It was always a higgledy-piggledy place. It was a standing joke in the family.

Jean looked horrified but everybody just laughed, even her Mum and Dad.

"Well you know me alright. I'm your exact opposite Louie."

Jean looked at the pair of them.

"So you are," she chimed out, "You're tall and thin, Mummy, and she's short and....."

"Let's change the subject, shall we," said Jack, hurriedly before Jean could finish the sentence.

The grown ups chatted nineteen to the dozen. Louie and Herbert stayed for dinner.

"You are lucky to have fresh eggs. We only get powdered eggs in London."

The unexpected guests were eating their boiled eggs with relish. Queenie began to cut Jean's bread into soldiers so that she could dip them into the lovely orange yolks.

"I can do it myself, Mum," protested Jean. She didn't want to appear babyish in front of the big girls.

Queenie smiled at Jack. "Sorry dear I forgot."

After tea Jack showed Herbert some of the changes to the farm they had made since Herbert's last visit.

Poppy and Margaret weren't very interested in the farm and so Jean just sat and stared at them sullenly.

At last it was time for them to leave to catch the train back to London. Jack took them to the station and Jean was glad when they left.

"You didn't tell me they were coming, Mummy."

"I didn't know they were coming. It's a bit of a game with Louie; she loves to catch me out."

"She's nosey!"

"Shush, that's rude."

"She can't hear me."

"You mustn't talk about people behind their backs."

Jean wasn't sure what that meant. She wanted to show Frank her conkers.

"Can I go to see Frank?"

"Change your clothes first!"

Jean rushed up to change again; back into the chicken soiled garments. She placed all the conkers in her pillow case and ran off to show Frank.

"Mum threw mine away."

"I hid mine in my drawer. I didn't half get ticked off when Mum found them. She thought they were alive."

They laughed and Joyce came up to see what was going on.

"Can I have some?" she pleaded.

Jean said she could spare two each and that she was going to plant the others.

Laurie let them plant six in his greenhouse. The others were planted in various situations; the copse, in the clearing where the bomb had dropped and two at the bottom of the garden near the cesspool. Those two grew enormously well. They soon got bored with planting so many and threw the rest away in the woods. The ones in the garden were over ten feet high within five years.

Jean went back home feeling very tired and went straight to bed. She dreamed of spies climbing trees and everyone was wearing a white dress except her.

During the Easter holidays the children explored the region between Staffhurst Wood and Edenbridge. They began by following the course of the River Jean. After this stream or brook's emergence in the thicket near the Nissan hut where the sentry post to the ammunition dump was situated, it flowed in a winding course through the brambles and along past the bomb crater. Although in most places, it was only a few inches deep, and about a yard wide, it was an attraction to Jean. The banks were covered in bright green moss, and the bottom of the stream bed was strewn with smooth colourful pebbles. Some of the little stones were round and some oval. Frank said that they were flint and her dad said that they had come here during the ice age. Some were broken and inside they were striped, yellow and brown. They had worn smooth with the endless tumbling they had endured in water over the centuries.

Scattered on the banks was a profusion of wild flowers, masses of celandine, some little purple violets, star like wood anemones, pretty yellow cowslips peeped out of their green velvet nests and in one place they found king-cups, growing in the water itself. The hazel nut trees hung their branches low over the tinkling stream, sometimes dangling low in the water and making eddies and sparkling ripples as the pale sunlight caught the water. Lots of birds nested near the water but their nests were so well camouflaged that the children rarely came upon them. Sometimes you could find the tell-tale droppings of the little wild rabbits, probable relatives of Bambi, Whiskers and Thumper.

Jean picked posies of wooden enemies for her mother but they always wilted before she got them home. Later in the year the red flowers would blossom; campion, ragged robin and willowherb would be abundant. The bracken thrust curled fronds out of the damp earth to spread by summer in dense layers under the trees.

One particular April afternoon, the three children and their dog set off to follow the river as far as they could go. They wore their wellies and raincoats as it had been raining for hours. The sun was hiding under a dull leaden sky and some big white clouds were visible high up over Crockham Hill. Each of these clouds, which were huge with wavy edges, had a halo of silver where the sun was trying to break through.

"Look at the clouds, Joyce! Aren't they beautiful?" Jean stared up at the magnificent sky.

"It's lovely. I wish I could draw it."

Joyce had been given a pencil set for Christmas.

"I am going to paint a picture of it when I get home."

"If you don't stop looking at the blooming sky, we'll have to go home before we've got anywhere," moaned Frank. "Get a move on. Renny is miles ahead of us."

The dog had run off along the river-bed. They had to navigate along the edges and were being hampered by the undergrowth.

"I'll tell Dad that you sweared at us."

"Let's walk in the water," said Jean, trying to keep the peace between brother and sister.

"Oh yeah! It will come over our boots," retorted Frank.

"We can get up on the bank when it gets too deep."

"Alright, we'll try it."

They got down in the little stream.

"OOH! I can feel the water. It's trying to get into my boots," squealed Jean.

It was true. The water was pushing against the rubber legs of their wellies as it rushed past them on its hurried journey to meet up with the River Eden. The water was not its usual clear colour either, it was muddy. There were lots of leaves and twigs rushing along in its clutches, like little boats at the mercy of the fast flowing water. The stream wound onwards and became wider as other little rivulets joined it from different sections in the woods.

"It's getting too deep for me," wailed Joyce as the water lapped near to the top of her boots.

"Climb up on the bank then," Frank ordered.

Joyce scrambled up the slippery slope of the clay bank and began to follow the other two adventurers who remained in the rushing stream. A few hundred yards further on, the stream disappeared into a small tunnel that went underneath the road. The three children stood on the bridge and leaned over the parapet watching the muddy water as it churned out of the dark tunnel.

They floated a few sticks from one side to another and ran back and forth across the road to watch their boats come out the other side.

They walked along beside someone's garden until the stream reached the edge of a field. The ground had recently been ploughed. The stream had been joined by others and was getting to be quite deep. Suddenly the little brook disappeared again, this time into a large, wide tunnel.

They had never been this far before.

"How deep is the water here?"

"Dunno."

"It looks very deep."

"I don't want to go in there", wailed Joyce.

"I do," said Jean.

"No one's going in today. It is far too deep after all the rain and anyway I think it's tea time," Frank said sensibly.

"Oh! Can't we ........" Jean's words were drowned out by a deafening noise. A rumbling sound that grew louder and louder and shook the very ground beneath their feet.

Joyce screamed.

# From Dragons to Ogres and Ice-cream.

Frank was speaking to them but his words were drowned by the thunder of the train rolling above them along the track. Jean burst into uncontrollable laughter at the sight of poor Joyce's face.

The train finally rumbled away.

"What on earth did you think it was Joyce?"

"I didn't know it was a train. It sounded like a dragon and I thought it was going to get me."

"It made me jump too, but only for a moment, and then I knew it was a train."

"Come on you two; it's getting late and we're miles from home."

"We could take a short cut."

"What short cut?" Frank demanded.

Jean thought and looked around her. She had a wonderful sense of direction and soon made up her mind. "We need to go that way," she pointed out across the ploughed field that arched above them like a burial mound. "We could save a mile if we don't follow the river. It has to go along the flat and if we go over that hill we ought to come out near the ghost station."

"What ghost station?" Joyce's voice quavered.

"I don't know why they call it that."

"I know where you mean," said Frank, wading up the steep sloping field.

It's a bit muddy," said Joyce, still a little worried.

"You're already muddy! A little bit more won't make any difference, Joyce."

They plodded up the hill treading in the deep furrows that the tractor had ploughed. It seemed very heavy going because the wet mud attached itself to their wellington boots.

Less than half way up Joyce got stuck. One of her boots would not come out of the mud. Frank and Jean took hold of her arms and pulled as hard as they could. With a squelch Joyce popped out of her sticky prison so suddenly that the other two fell over backwards and Joyce fell on her face. However, the Wellington boot was still there, stuck tight in the mud.

The three of them sat there in the wet brown earth and looked at each other.

"We're in for a hiding when Dad sees the state of us."

Joyce began to cry and wiped her tears with her hands. She sat there looking so dismal that Jean began to laugh. Frank joined in, and finally Joyce saw the funny side of it too. They retrieved the "Blasted Boot" as Frank called it and the trio clambered on up to the top of the mound. The dog leapt about barking.

It was very dark overhead and the clouds were exceptionally low. It began to rain. Huge, heavy drops which became heavier as the heavens opened and the rain fell in sheets. The mud began to dribble off the children as the water ran down off their bare heads like a waterfall. As if by magic it washed their faces clean.

They ran off homewards, holding hands and shouting through the noise of the downpour.

Luckily their sense of direction never failed. There were no road names to go by as these had been removed to prevent enemy parachutists landing in Britain from finding their way.

It only took about half an hour to reach the farm and Jean suggested that they all go in to her house first.

Standing on the back door step trying to get out of their wellies and shivering with cold, they looked a sorry sight.

Queenie took one look and dragged them in out of the cold. Renny bounded in as well and before Queenie could stop him he gave his entire body a gigantic dog shake and showered everyone with doggy raindrops. Then he loped over to the hearth and plonked down in front of the kitchen fire. Tubby, who had been ensconced happily there, arched his back, spat at the dog and shot off.

"Just look at you poor little mites. Quickly jump out of those wet clothes. Frank, go upstairs and wrap a blanket around yourself. You can have a bath after the girls."

She took the girls up to the bathroom and ran a nice hot bath. The poor little mites scrambled into the bath and sunk into the lovely warm water. Queenie soaped them all over with pink carbolic. Then she washed their hair and they didn't even cry when the soap got in their eyes.

At last, all three of them were wrapped in toasty warm towels.

Tubby was sulking on the window ledge with his back towards everyone. Only his ears betrayed him; they were pointed backwards towards the people and the horrid dog who had usurped his place in front of the fire.

The children drank their cocoa sitting on the settee in front of the ideal boiler. The settee had seen better days. It was made of wood and had once possessed soft corduroy cushions in light brown but they had worn out. Jack had replaced them with the back seat of an old car. These new seats were made of mock leather with springs inside and were very bouncy. They lasted for years after the war before Jack could be persuaded to buy a new suite of furniture.

Queenie wrinkled her nose.

"What's that funny smell?"

"I can't smell anything," said Frank.

"I can and it's Renny! He stinks!"

"No he doesn't, Mummy; he always smells like that. It's just doggy-smell."

"Well he can go outside and smell in the garden," she retorted as she endeavoured to shift him. The steam was rising off his lovely red coat and he lay all limp so that Queenie couldn't move him at all.

"Oh bother," she muttered. "He's a dead weight."

Tubby was watching with interest, waiting to return to the fire. At last, Renny got up and mooched to the door. It had stopped raining and Queenie threw the dog out.

By the time she got back, Tubby was curled up asleep by the fire. The smell of dog lingered for days.

Queenie told Doris that the children had been caught in the storm.

The trio looked at each other in relief. Queenie had put their clothes ready to wash.

"You won't need them tomorrow. I expect you will be stopping indoors!"

Jean went to sit with Tubby.

"You know I love you best, Tubby," she consoled him.

Tubby began to purr.

She stroked him and he purred even louder.

After tea Jack and Queenie turned the radio on to hear the six o'clock news.

"The Russians have reached Berlin and are waiting for the American army, said the voice of the wireless.

Jean knew him as Alvarleedell.

"The war will soon be over I think. It's only a matter of time."

"You said that ages ago Mummy."

"Just wait until they get their hands on that ruddy Hitler," said Jack, who was rubbing his weather beaten hands together.

"I just want everything to get back to normal. No more rationing, decent clothes to wear, coffee, ice cream...."

"What is ice cream like?" Jean interrupted.

"It is the most delicious tasting pudding in the world."

Jean looked puzzled.

"But what is it like?"

"It is cream that has been frozen and it is really sweet and cold. It is a really delicious dessert."

"What is a dessert?"

"It is a posh word for pudding," said Jack.

"You mean afters," said Jean. "Is it like when the milk gets frozen in the bottle and pops up out of the top?"

"Very similar," said Queenie. "Ice cream was available in hotels before the war. It has to be kept in a refrigerator."

"A what?"

That's rather hard to explain. The hotels have big cupboards which use gas to freeze food and then it doesn't go bad. In America some ordinary people have refrigerators."

"It's one of those new-fangled American gadgets," said Jack disdainfully. "I can't see them catching on in England."

"After the war I will buy you an ice cream cake for your birthday." Queenie laughed and gave Jean a big hug.

"And now it's time for bed. Up you go."

She gave Jean a little push towards the stairs. "I'll be up in a minute to tuck you in."

Tubby led the way up to his bedroom and Jean tumbled into bed. Then she remembered to say her prayers.

"God bless Mummy and Daddy and Tubby and Susan and Renny and Grandma and the cousins and everybody else," she mumbled quickly. "And look after all the soldiers too, especially Uncle Alf."

As she lay there she tried to imagine how ice cream tasted and fell asleep with a little smile on her face.

The next day dawned just like any other and Jean pottered around the farm helping her father and uncle. They had just finished mucking out the cowsheds when Queenie appeared at the top of the path yelling and waving her arms about.

"Quickly, come up here all of you!" she yelled at the top of her voice.

Jack dropped his big broom, and fearing that something dreadful had happened to his mother, he ran up to the house at top speed.

What ever could have happened to make his wife act so agitated, he wondered?

His brother Frank whizzed up after him and Jean trudged along behind, realizing that she had got her school clothes dirty.

Queenie and Jack's mother were standing in the kitchen with tears pouring down their cheeks.

"What the hell is wrong?"

"He's dead! He's really dead!" Queenie was crying and laughing all at once.

"It's true!" Emily Pearce chimed in, rubbing tears from wrinkled eyes with the corner of her apron.

"Who?" Both men yelled.

"Hitler!" The two women and Jack and Frank flung their arms around each other and began to dance a kind of jig together.

Everyone was laughing and cheering and Jean stared and stared. Had they gone mad? She wondered.

"What is it?" She tugged at Queenie's skirt.

Jack bent down and swept her up in his arms and held her high above his head until she nearly hit the rafters.

"Old man Hitler is dead," he bellowed.

"He didn't exactly die." Queenie explained. "He committed suicide. It came over the wireless just now."

"Maybe there's some more news."

The grown ups gathered around the precious Philco and listened intently to the voice of a man.

Jean went off in search of her cousins. Doris was rushing up the path.

Jean knew that it must be good news but was too young to realise the full implications. She had never, ever, seen her parents so happy, let alone Uncle Frank who was normally a very quiet man. He didn't smile much as a rule.

She saw Frank and Joyce coming round the corner and ran to meet them.

"Have you HEARD?" Frank yelled.

"Yes. Hitler has done something."

"He killed himself. That news reader said so."

"How do they know?"

"I'm not sure, but my mum says that the war will end now."

"That's good; now we are all going to get ice cream."

"What?" Frank gave her a funny look.

"The only reason we can't have really nice food is because of the war but I'm not sure why though."

"I know," said Frank, using his I'm cleverer than you voice. "It's because some food doesn't grow here and has to come by sea."

"Well?"

"The Germans keep sinking all the ships."

"Oh, I get it," said Jean.

Suddenly it all became clear to her.

"The ships have got all the ice cream, bananas and chocolates and stuff like that on board," Jean explained to Joyce.

"The rotten lot; they must want to eat it all themselves," Joyce retorted.

"I bet that's just what happens!"

The penny had dropped. Jean suddenly realised what the war was all about.

"I bet Germany is full of lovely, lovely food. They pinched all ours!" She shouted out.

"Yeah, and now he's dead, we'll get it all back."

"Yeah! Hooray!" The three children cheered.

Between them, the youngsters thought they had sorted it all out, and they trotted up the path to join the adults.

Bursting into the kitchen, they were all talking at once.

"Can we have ice cream tomorrow?"

"When will the bananas arrive; and you'll soon be able to have coffee, Mum?"

Queenie had practically suffered withdrawal symptoms when coffee supplies ran-out. It was available on the black-market but at exorbitant prices. Jean had never drunk coffee but imagined that it was delicious. She hated tea; it tasted bitter and nasty. Her father took to standing a teapot on the hot surface of the ideal boiler. This kept the brew hot for when he popped in for a drink during the day. The whole kitchen stank of it until Queenie threw it away and made a fresh brew.

The smell of it was enough to put Jean off tea for the rest of her life.

"Will we get a day off school?"

"The war is not over yet, I'm afraid," said Jack soberly.

Silence fell on the room.

"Cheer up though. It won't be long now."

"No, that is for sure. Those Huns won't last long without their damn dictator."

The children stared at Jack, who very rarely swore.

"Ooh," said Joyce.

Jack just chuckled. "If it lasts another week I'll be surprised."

"Perhaps it will be over by your birthday?" said Doris.

"I couldn't ask for a better present."

Just then, everyone heard a clip clopping noise on the path outside. Queenie went to the back door and screamed.

"The cows are coming in!"

"Oh damn; I must have forgotten to close the gate," cursed Frank.

Jack and Frank rounded up the cows and shooed them back to the field. The big animals began bucking and swaying around in their ungainly way; trampling the garden under their hooves, but nobody grumbled. Beauty charged the washing on the line. She scooped up a pillowcase on one horn and then she made her way back to the field. The others followed her.

"Let's all have a cup of tea?" said Queenie in relief.

She ran the water into the big brown kettle and put it on the top of the kitchen range; thinking that after the war she'd like to buy one of the new-fangled American electric kettles. A smile lit her face. Jack would argue that they didn't need one but she'd win. It was going to be so different; just like the old days only better. The three women drunk their tea and the children wandered off after the men. Tubby followed at a distance, in case that dog or maybe a left over cow was nearby.

There was an air of anticipation hanging over the whole country for the next few days. People the length and breadth of the British Isles, not to mention the rest of free Europe, were glued to their wireless sets; eager for any more news regarding the downfall of Germany.

Gradually news arrived about Hitler's final hours. Some said that he had hidden in a bunker with his mistress Eva Braun. It seemed that they had both committed suicide. Other reports said that he had married Eva Braun first. His body was missing. Most people didn't care one way or another so long as he was really and truly dead. Others wondered if he really was dead, or had he made his escape. This theory remained in most people's minds for many years. Hitler had been so wicked that many could just not believe that he was indeed dead. They thought that he might be hiding in South America.

Jean thought secretly for a long time that he could still be alive. She was still a little scared of the green curtain that fell in leg shaped folds, in case that was where he might be hiding. She also knew that he was clever enough to vanish quickly if anybody pulled the curtain back. Then, of course, he would hide somewhere else.

Many years later, when Queenie finally disposed of the old curtain, a much older Jean felt a strange sense of relief. She had forgotten that it was that very curtain that had saved her life, the day all the bombs fell. The debris from upstairs had become entangled in the heavy curtain instead of falling upon Jean, who was sitting on the floor nearby.

"Well, two down and one to go," said Jack. "Now let's get rid of that Jap fellow and things will be great again."

Benito Mussolini was also dead. In 1944 after being deposed, but whilst trying to flee from Italy into Switzerland, he and his mistress were both shot dead.

"He was only a blacksmith's son, you know. How he ever got to be their President I'll never know." Jack declared.

It was said later that the two bodies were taken from Lake Como, where they had been shot, to Milan where the people came to view the corpses hanging upside down in the main square, so that there was no doubt about their deaths.

"What a pity that they didn't do the same thing to Hitler. There's no proof that he's dead."

"I didn't realise that you were so barbaric." Queenie said with a smile.

Jean's gaze slid over towards the green curtain and she shuddered at the sight of a pairs of boots peeping from underneath. I know that they are Daddy's, she told herself sternly.

"Why did Mussolini became a fascist?" Queenie mused.

"Probably got the idea from one of his cronies in the Police or some of those Commies he met up with when he was a journalist."

Queenie had a quick mental picture of her friends Charles and Lulu whispering in secret to the fat old Mussolini. She chuckled out loud. It had been fashionable in the twenties to join the Communist party and many young people had done so, and regretted it later.

"What are you laughing about old girl?"

"Oh nothing at all really, and less of the "old girl" thank you very much. I wonder what will happen in Europe now."

"I don't care; we've got to get this country in order first."

"When the men come home there will be plenty for them to do. Look at the devastation in London."

Jack and Queenie sat up long into the night.

Jean was straining her ears in case she missed something.

"Hey you, sleepy-head, it's time you were in bed."

"Let me stay up."

"You'll never wake up for school."

Tubby purred gently in her ear until she dropped off into a dream world where there were all kinds of wondrous food available. Unfortunately, none of it had any taste whatsoever.

The next day was sunny and bright. The children were home for half term and were playing cricket in the field when they became aware of smoke rising into the sky from the vicinity of the railway. They ran helter-skelter to see what was on fire. Uncle Frank wasn't far behind them. When they reached the railway embankment they saw the flames. Obviously a cinder from the engine had set the grass alight.

"It could get worse and spread into the field and I don't want to lose the hay," said Uncle Frank. "Run home and ask Granny to telephone the station and tell them to come and put it out."

The children ran back and relayed the message.

Granny Pearce got muddled up and instead of phoning the Railway Station, she phoned the Fire Station. The children ran back to watch the fire as it spread along the bank. Uncle Frank stamped on any stray flames that encroached into the hay field. Suddenly they heard a strange noise; it sounded like bells and it was getting louder all the time. Frank had been expecting some railway men to come along the track but instead, two fire engines arrived and Granny let them in through the top gate. A large red fire engine and a smaller grey one careered across the first field, their bells ringing deafeningly. The two vehicles circled the hay field and arrived noisily at the fence.

Uncle Frank was amazed and embarrassed. He apologized to the firemen and explained the mistake.

"Don't worry about it. This is the biggest fire we've had for weeks," said the Chief. "We get chimney fires and cats up trees but this is the real Mckoy."

They soon had the fire under control and off went the fire engines with Frank and Joyce and Jean riding on board as far as the gate.

"Wasn't that smashing?" shouted Frank.

"Good old Granny," Jean shouted back as they waved the firemen goodbye.

The strange thing was that after that incident, Jean had a recurring dream on and off for the rest of her life. In the dream, the woods next to the house were ablaze and the houses were in danger. It was always a relief to wake up and find it wasn't real.

# Starlight and Sanity.

Jean's new friend Ann Lever had been playing with her and it was arranged that Ann could stay at Jean's house to sleep that night. The children smuggled bits of food upstairs and raided the sweet jar for a midnight feast. They ate it all before midnight however. Little did they know what was about to happen the next day. They were awoken by the sound of the wireless blaring out the next morning.

Queenie rushed in to break the news; the war was over, peace had been declared.

Germany surrendered to the Allies in May 1945, and after almost six long years, the Second World War was over. After Queenie left them, the two girls were whooping and cheering out of the window of Jean's bedroom. Frank appeared outside and instead of going running downstairs Ann and Jean clambered out of the window and slid down the roof to perch on the top of the flat bay window. From there they leapt off and landed on the front lawn, winded a little but elated. The three children ran around cheering and talking nineteen to the dozen about what would happen now. After breakfast the two girls went down the road to Ann's house as Ann wanted to see if her Mum had heard the news. Of course she had and more celebrating took place in Red Lane Cottages.

Of course there was universal rejoicing; Londoners congregated in the war torn streets celebrating long into the night.

In the countryside life went on as usual, the cows got milked and the eggs were collected. Some things were different however and the thing that Jean liked best was the discontinuation of the use of blackout curtains.

That first night, as it got really dark, Queenie went to draw the heavy black kitchen curtains, before putting the lights on. Then she realised that it wasn't necessary any more. She looked up at the Caxton Home for Printers and further along, the Seaman's Home. Each of the lovely buildings had all their electric lights on, blazing out triumphantly across the valley. As she watched, more lights sprang up all across the hillside. Each home proclaimed Victory and Peace by lighting up the whole valley.

"Jack! Jean! Come into the kitchen; hurry." The excitement made her voice sound high and squeaky.

"What is it?" Jack began and stopped suddenly as he too saw the lights twinkling, all over the hillside.

His voice choked and he saw the tears of happiness flowing in uncontrollable rivers down his wife's cheeks; tears of happiness and joy. He hugged her and his own salt tears joined hers.

"What is it?" Jean tugged at their clothes. Although almost nine, she was too small to see out of the high window. Jack scooped her up and pointed to the distant horizon.

"Look!"

Jean looked out of the window, and for the first time in her life, she saw the lights from the other houses scattered all across the hillside. They shone like a million glow-worms.

"It's beautiful. Let's put our lights on too."

Queenie ran across to the light switch and pressed the little knob down.

The white light shone out across the fields illuminating the trees and the whole valley, uniting with the rest of the gleaming, shining electric or gas lights from all the houses across Limpsfield Chart.

They were proclaiming that Britain had triumphed at last and that her people never would be slaves of the Germans!

Finally Jean and her beloved cat lay in bed with the windows open, listening and watching the night.

Jack and Queenie sat on her bed for a while. Jack showed the little girl her first glimpse of yet another wonder; the night sky. Stars in their millions were twinkling in the inky heavens.

How wonderful it was to lie in her bed up under the eaves and stare up at the Milky Way. She had never before seen the stars in all their glory. They had been there all the time, oblivious of the war, shining out over a world too scared to look at them.

"The stars have names, Jean," said Jack. "Look over there; can you make out five stars quite a distance apart that form the letter M lying on its side; just there," he pointed up and drew the letter with his fingertips for Jean.

"Yes, I see them," she whispered, staring at the formation.

"That is called a constellation. It has a name too; those five stars are called Cassiopeia."

"What a funny name."

"The ancient astronomers called the stars and constellations after Greek Gods."

"What gods, Daddy? What is a stronamer?"

"We'll talk about all that another day."

"Do all the stars have names? What is that very bright one hanging over the hill called?" Jean pointed to the north.

"That's Capella, and that constellation shaped like a saucepan is called The Plough." He began to tell her names of the constellations.

"Aren't they bright? What makes them shine?"

" Hey! Settle down it's time to go to sleep. Wait until the winter and I'll show you some beauties like Orion the Hunter and his dog."

"Show me now!" The eager child cried out.

"I can't. Orion isn't in our sky right now."

"Where is it?"

"Some stars, like Orion, are shining on the other side of the World in Australia at this time of year."

Jack tried to explain about the shift of the heavens but it was a bit too much for Jean to take in.

However, the night sky became a passion for her and she studied it in books. Even years later, when she was a Grandmother herself, when she looked out of the kitchen window and saw the bright lights of the big houses on the opposite hillside, she remembered a strange happy feeling in the pit of her stomach.

Many years after her parents died, Jean was to stand alone in the big kitchen, remembering that day wistfully. She would get a strange feeling as if something amazing was about to happen. It always reminded her of that glorious night, when the war ended. It was a wonderful reminder of her childhood when she and her parents had celebrated the victory night together.

A few months later, the war against Japan ended abruptly with the dropping of the terrible Atom Bomb.

Jean expected everything to change immediately but life went on in pretty much the same way.

It was another three years, by the way, before any of the children got their first taste of ice cream. Jean and Valerie were at the grammar school by then and aged twelve. News came through the grapevine that Boynes sweet shop would have some ice cream for sale one Monday.

The queue of children reached from the shop near the railway entrance for several hundred yards round the corner and as far as Tandridge Motor Centre. .

One brick of ice cream per child was the ration. Jean ate it all and then sucked the soggy blue and yellow wrapping paper.

She had her first banana milk shake in Cornwall the same year. In fact she had three in one afternoon and then she was sick. She has not had one since.

When Jean was fifteen, her Godfather asked her to visit him in Germany. He was a padre in the army during the period after the war when the allies were stationed there. It was there, in that defeated country, that Jean ate her first Black Forest Gateaux and other scrumptious desserts. These delicious cakes and pastries had still not hit the grocery shelves in England. It did seem a little odd to her. Food rationing lasted longer in Britain than in Germany.

She remembered telling her cousins that Hitler had stolen all their ice-cream; perhaps he had stolen all the recipe books as well.

### THE END

# Epilogue

To Chris and Frankie.

As I write this record of my childhood during that war, I can still picture my Mum and Dad, your Grandma and Grandfather stoically endeavouring to make my childhood a happy one despite the hostility abroad. Whenever I look across towards the hills of Limpsfield Chart, I feel that they are both watching over us all. They will be in my heart and my everlasting memory. I know that you remember them too; they loved you both dearly.

That is why I want you to read about my memories of those war years.

I hope that none of you have to experience a World War for if it happens again, it will be much more terrible than my war was.

It is now over sixty years since the war ended and my memory is a little blurred.

Tubby, my beautiful ginger cat, and companion for twenty years, died in my arms at the ripe old age of twenty. I was twenty-one and I missed him terribly.

Mum.

## A Mother's Love

Though many years have slipped away
I see your beauty as before.
And in the twilight of my days
I know you're waiting by the door.

There is no love so deep and true
As from a mother to her child
Until its time to come to you
Oh Mummy, I must bide a while
To cherish babies you once knew
Who still remember your sweet smile?

So wait for me and do not pine
Now Daddy's there to help you through,
And hold your hand until its time
For little Jean to come to you.

To my parents who passed away too soon

# About the Author

Jean Pearce Edwards began writing when she retired from her job as a sales manager and has since had three novels published.

She was born in Edenbridge but has lived in Staffhurst Wood, Limpsfield on a small farm for most of her life. Although the farm was sold in the fifties, her family kept the farmhouse. Jean still lives in the house her father built and would never dream of moving away.

She is married to John and they have a son, Chris, a daughter Francesca, and a granddaughter Megan.

Jean attended Merle Common Primary School and Oxted County Grammar School. She hoped to become a teacher and went to college in Yorkshire but hated it.

Many local women know her as the Avon Lady as she once went door to door selling Avon cosmetics. Once she swapped her motorbike for a car, she advanced to being the manager for that company and did very well

Her hobbies include gardening, traveling to ancient ruins around the globe, and aqua-aerobics at Edenbridge Leisure Centre, which keep her fit!!!

As a youngster at school she excelled at sport and hated lessons. She went on to represent Great Britain in the high jump event; thanks to her father's training and Mr Sutton, the P.E master at

Oxted who saw her potential. Her proudest moment was marching with the English Commonwealth

Games Athletic Team at the Games in 1958.

This story is not like the others because it was simply written to tell her family what her childhood was like; back in the "good old days."

She is writing a fifth novel which is the prequel to Dreamkill.

She would like to thank everyone who has said that they enjoyed the first three novels.

Lightning Source UK Ltd.
Milton Keynes UK
16 February 2010

150131UK00001B/4/P

9 781434 391339